# Babies
# It's Warm
# Inside

# Babies
# It's Warm
# Inside

---

## LIA FARRELL

CAMEL
PRESS
Kenmore, WA

Epicenter Press
6524 NE 181st St.
Suite 2
Kenmore, WA 98028

www.epicenterpress.com
www.camelpress.com
www.coffeetownpress.com

For more information go to: www.liafarrell.net

Cover design by Dawn Anderson

ISBN: 9781603818162 (Trade Paper)
ISBN: 9781941890837 (eBook)

Produced in the United States of America

This book is dedicated to Molly Fiona. Known as "Fee" she was Lyn's True Companion who helped her through the early years after losing her husband. Fee left us in March, 2019 having never lost her dauntless personality and loving spirit.

# PROLOGUE

———

A TEENAGE BOY IN A DENIM JACKET was walking toward her, looking intently at his phone. She had just emerged from the florist shop and was carrying a bouquet of white roses. He didn't see her coming towards him. She stared at the teen-ager, willing him to look up. By the time it became obvious that he wasn't going to, it was too late. His shoulder slammed into her. Hard. She winced. At her age, that would leave a nasty bruise.

"Look where you're going, Lady," he snarled. After a brief glance, his eyes were riveted on his cellphone once more.

"Excuse me!" She yelled at his retreating back. "I was looking where I was going... Oh, never mind."

She looked around at the other passersby on the crowded sidewalk of the town where she was born and had lived for most of her life and felt a chill. She didn't recognize a soul. No one even gave her so much as a sympathetic glance.

*I was a ballerina once. I pirouetted in the spotlight. People cheered and gave me flowers. They saw me.*

She made her way home slowly. The gracious old house where she was born welcomed her as it always did. She lived with ghosts, but they were kindly spirits. Her mother seemed to sit at the piano, straight-backed, hands resting lightly on the keys. Her father looked up from the newspaper he was reading with a faint smile on his thin face. Henry, handsome as a movie star, beckoned to her from the hallway. He'd enlisted after medical school and went straight to Vietnam from their honeymoon, never to return.

That had been a dark time. She didn't have the heart to pursue her ballet career and returned to the familiar surroundings of her small, southern hometown and the comforting presence of parents and friends. Rosedale welcomed her back with open arms, and she began teaching ballet in her mother's studio. Thirty-some years later, her mother died of cancer and her father was gone within a year. Once again, she had been comforted and sustained by her community. Shaking her head, she looked around the darkening room.

"There's something wrong here," she whispered. "But what can I do?"

Without answering, her ghosts faded away. She was alone.

# ONE

FOR THE BETTER PART OF AN HOUR, Ben Bradley, Sheriff of Rose County, had been trying to work out a Thanksgiving dinner location with his heavily pregnant wife, Mae. The couple had been married for less than a year, but his bride wanted children and had gotten pregnant shortly after their wedding in March. Ever since the day Mae informed him that she was expecting twins, Ben had felt a growing sense of trepidation, fearful he would be unequal to the task of combining fatherhood with his demanding job as Sheriff of Rose County. Even though Mae's due date wasn't until January third, he was aware that twins often came early and worried constantly that he would be unreachable, chasing some criminal when she went into labor.

"I think it would make sense for us to have Thanksgiving dinner with my folks, Mae. It's getting close to your due date and my mom is a nurse. They live near the hospital and if you went into labor, she would be on site and could help," Ben said.

"You know my original plan was to have Thanksgiving dinner in our house and include both sets of families," Mae said, looking wistfully around their updated farmhouse kitchen. "But my doctor drew the line. He said he was tempted to make me go to bed for the remainder of the pregnancy and absolutely forbid me from making dinner for sixteen people."

"Sixteen. How did you get to that number?" Ben frowned.

"Two sets of parents, my sister, her husband and their three children, your brother and his family, plus the three of us, including your son. That's sixteen, unless you also wanted to include your former fiancé and my predecessor, Matt's biological mother," Mae gave him a mischievous grin and Ben shook his head.

"Well, regardless of the number, clearly we aren't having it here. It's only a week away. So, what about going to my folks?"

"You know I love your parents, but as the date gets closer, I find myself feeling just a little bit… apprehensive about the birth. My sister, July, had twins and between her and my mother, I think I'd feel more relaxed there. And my parents have more space at their house."

"Okay, that's it then. Can't have my beautiful and very pregnant wife fretful," Ben hugged Mae as best he could with her expanded waistline and gave her a kiss on the forehead. "I have to get to work, Honey. I'll call you later."

AFTER DRIVING THROUGH THE VILLAGE of Rosedale and seeing that all was quiet, Ben parked his truck at the sheriff's office. Miss Dory Clarkson, the African American "Czarina" of the place, was waiting for him in the open doorway. She was wearing a trench coat, having obviously just arrived. Her arms were crossed over her chest and she was tapping her fingers on her arms, an irritated look on her face.

"You certainly took your time getting here this morning," she said as Ben reached the door. "I assume you managed to forget today's important meeting while coddling your pregnant wife. As big as she is, it doesn't look to me like it'll be long before Mae has those babies."

"She's getting pretty tired of being pregnant, that's for sure," Ben said, walking into the waiting room of the office. The building was a time capsule from the fifties, with fluorescent lights that flickered and brown linoleum tile on the floor.

"I'm glad to see you wore your uniform today, Sheriff. Makes you look more official. The budget meeting starts at six," Dory said. "You have work to do before the County Commissioner arrives with his usual request for budget cuts."

"Fine. We can meet in the conference room in an hour. I'd like the whole staff there."

"Well, you're pretty much looking at it. Rob is attending his Field Officer course as you know. Deputy George is patrolling the rural roads of the county, probably stopping at every restaurant hoping for female admiration, which is likely to be in short supply," Dory raised an eloquent eyebrow. "Mrs. Coffin has taken the day off for dentist and doctor appointments, Deputy Cam is out with the flu and Detective Nichols is in the wind."

Ben sighed and walked down the hall toward his office. Sitting at his battered desk, he picked up a framed photograph of Mae holding a puppy. She had a look of total adoration on her face. The picture reminded him of the day he had first met the girl who became his lovely wife. She had come into the office to report her neighbor, Ruby Mead Allison, missing— all the while holding a wiggling tote bag on her lap.[1] The tote contained a dog belonging to the missing woman. He later learned she ran a dog boarding business called "Mae's Place". Even with her damp, tousled hair and casual clothes, she was downright gorgeous. He remembered casting a surreptitious look at her left hand, pleased to see that she wasn't wearing a ring.

Mae had history with the sheriff's office, he found out later. Her father, Don December, had served as the police photographer for many years and her journalist mother, Suzanne, often hung around the place hoping for tidbits for 'Suzanne about Town', a column she wrote for the local Rosedale paper. It had been a momentous two and a half years since they met. Shortly after meeting Mae, Ben had discovered he had a son, Matthew. The boy's mother, Ben's former fiancé Katie Hudson, had broken off their engagement abruptly and eloped with a man she barely knew. Little Matt was a toddler and Katie was divorced before she got around to telling Ben

1 Farrell, Lia, One Dog Too Many, Camel Press, 2013.

about his son's existence. Katie had since returned to Rosedale and they shared custody of Matt—who was now in first grade.

When they first started dating, Ben had been introduced to Mae's dog-boarding life. In return, Mae wanted to be involved in investigating cases with him. It had been a difficult transition, but ultimately, they had solved several murders together and he had learned to value her insights. When Ben was initially appointed Acting Sheriff, he was still trying to decide whether to go to law school or continue police work. Meeting Mae, falling in love and a landslide election victory had made him realize his true calling. He cut his mental reminiscences short, hearing Dory's heels click down the hall as she entered the conference room.

Miss Dory Clarkson had shed her trench coat to reveal a fitted navy sheath, copper jewelry and gray, high-heeled shoes. Such tight clothing should have looked inappropriate on her senior body, but somehow, she pulled it off. She had worked for the sheriff's office for almost fifty years, beginning as a teen-ager. As the iron hand in a velvet glove, she often elicited a "Yes ma'am" even from their curmudgeonly senior detective. Her energy was undimmed after decades of ordering them all about, which she maintained they sorely needed. Ben reluctantly turned his attention to the papers Dory was placing on the table. Picking up a stapled bundle he skimmed the dense budgetary information.

"I see that you and Mrs. Coffin have proposed three percent increases for all the personnel, which is standard for county employees. I suppose it would be too much to ask for an actual budget increase this year, beyond the cost of living and a new patrol car. There's no choice on that. I guess I ought to thank George for totaling the old one."

"Boss, I've been hearing rumors that we're going to be asked to take a big cut this year," Dory said, looked at him seriously.

"Damn it. We're expected to be cops, marriage counselors, psychologists, medical first responders and security guards. As law enforcement is asked to do more and more, we're somehow supposed to do so with less funding. I'm not going to agree to that today. No way." He shook his head. "Sheriffs have to consent to the proposed budget, you know."

"Be that as it may, according to scuttlebutt the state has done some sort of crime analysis and Rose County has the lowest crime rate of any county in Tennessee, except for the murders which have been explained away as anomalies—non-recurrent crimes of passion."

"I'm aware, but the reason the crime rate is low is because we've done our jobs so well! I hate reducing all of our hard work to numbers."

"Well, don't shoot the messenger. Just prepare your arguments and try not to completely piss off the commissioner and his minions."

"Fine," Ben said shortly. "I assume our Under Sheriff, Detective Rob, will be back from Field Officer training in time for the budget debacle?" When Dory nodded, he picked up his cell phone and called Mae.

"Miss me already?" her sweet voice greeted him.

"You know it, Honey. I'm sorry but there's a budget meeting tonight at six. It'll probably take about two hours for me to pull out my weapon and brain the County Commissioner with it. Might need you to give me an alibi, say you went into labor early or something. Just kidding. I'll be home after the meeting, probably between eight and nine. Are you taking it easy?"

"Yes. I'm sitting here on the back porch thinking about the first time we sat in these chairs. It was the evening you came over to tell me to stop meddling in Ruby Mead Allison's murder case. I remember asking you to stay and whether you wanted a drink. I said you looked like you needed one. Our lives have certainly been a wild ride since then. Oh, I got a call from Katie. She's bringing your son over on Monday night. He'll be with us through Thanksgiving. He wants to see the dogs," she laughed.

"And the two of us, I would hope," Ben said. "Are you sure you're up to it?"

"Of course. Stop fretting, worrywart, I'll be fine."

"Okay, I'll text you later with my ETA."

# TWO

———

COUNTY COMMISSIONER KURT JENSEN, who looked like a lumberjack with his bushy red beard, and his two assistants, Janey and Bob (so young they looked like middle-schoolers to Ben) were escorted into the conference room at six on the dot. Ben could hear Sophie Coffin, their office manager and dispatcher asking them if they wanted their coffee leaded or unleaded. She had also purchased sandwiches for the meeting. They declined everything. *Probably a bad sign.* Ben got up from his desk. Taking a deep breath and straightening his shoulders, he walked down the hall.

"Sheriff," the commissioner said formally, nodding at Ben as Janey handed him a stapled packet of paper.

"Commissioner," Ben replied dryly. Normally the proposed budget Dory and Mrs. Coffin prepared was the only document at the meeting. *A commissioner's budget proposal didn't bode well.*

Ben's Under Sheriff, Detective Rob Fuller, entered the room. He was slim, wore silver-rimmed glasses and was dressed in his brown uniform. The two of them were the only representatives of the office staff at the meeting. Ben's Senior Detective, Wayne Nichols, had called earlier in the day. He had tentatively offered to attend the meeting, but admitted he dreaded that sort of thing. Dory begged off, too. Deputy

George Phelps was guarding the sole prisoner in the jail, a drunk and disorderly well known to the staff. Mrs. Coffin had come in to handle the phones and dispatch.

"Let's get started. Please be seated, everyone," Ben said.

"I apologize for not getting this to you earlier," Kurt Jensen said. "We just finished it. If you'll take a look at page four, you'll see the bottom line. I'm sorry, but we have to cut your budget by almost fifteen percent."

"What!" Ben exclaimed. "Fifteen percent? A cut like that will decimate my staff. I only have eight people working for me, including our office manager and two lab techs, and more than eighty percent of my budget is tied up in salaries. It's totally unacceptable." Ben felt his face get red and a storm of less-than-polite words rising to the surface before Rob laid a hand on his shoulder.

"Excuse us please, Commissioner," Rob said. "This is all new information and we need a moment to discuss it." He kept his hand on Ben's arm. "May we have the room?" Rob smiled at Janey, who dimpled back at him, and the three county employees departed.

"Okay, take a deep breath. Can I get you anything?" Rob asked.

"A stiff drink," Ben growled under his breath.

"I'm about to say something you're going to want to belt me for, but having been Under Sheriff since you got married last spring, I think you should consider agreeing to some budget cuts."

"What the hell, Rob?" Ben's face flushed. His fists were clenched.

"Hold on, Ben. Just hear me out. We're top-heavy, overstaffed in the upper ranks and understaffed at the patrol and deputy levels," Rob took an uneven breath. "We have two detectives and a senior investigator but only two deputies."

"Go on," Ben bit off his words.

"We both know that Rose County is one of the safest places in the Middle South and practically in the whole country. It's a testament to the great job we're doing, but what we don't have are enough deputies for patrol or any officers to cover other emerging areas. We have no dedicated drug unit or school liaison person and I shudder to think that there could be a school shooting with only George on site. All he does is flirt with the school lunch ladies and sneak cafeteria food." Rob shook his head. "We're covering a three hundred plus square-mile county and protecting nearly fifteen thousand citizens with only two deputies. Lately both you and I have been pulling patrol duty just to cover the clock. We've totally abandoned giving out parking or speeding tickets downtown. Plus, we need an IT person. The office needs to have its security upgraded. Last week my little sister hacked into our database."

The head of steam Ben had built up was draining away. "Your little sister? Seriously? Isn't she in high school?" Rob nodded. Ben took a deep breath and said, "Okay, what's your idea then?"

"If both Dory and Wayne retired, we could hire three more officers as well as get a dedicated IT person. Plus, I've been researching grants and think I've found one that we can apply for to upgrade our computer equipment. It's not a done deal, but I'm willing to write the grant if you accept the budget cuts and ask for resignations from Dory and Wayne." Their eyes met and Ben gave a reluctant nod.

Two HOURS LATER, AFTER A drawn-out negotiating session, the sheriff's budget for the year was approved with "only" a ten percent cut. Ben thanked Rob for his input and helping him keep a lid on his temper and left the office heading for home. He called Mae from his truck. By the time Ben got to Little Chapel Road and pulled up the hill to park in their driveway, he was calmer but still ready for that drink. He went inside and heard Mae's voice call him from the back porch.

"I'm out here, Ben. I've got a bottle of Chianti, plus steaks ready to go on the grill."

"Come here, you," Ben said pulling all of Mae into his arms.

"It was a long tough day and we didn't even get any reports of crime in the whole county."

"I know," she said and kissed him. "Rob called and told me that you're going to have to lay off some staff. I'm sorry."

"It looks like Wayne and Dory are going to have to go. The thought is tearing me apart. I doubt I'll be able to sleep tonight."

"Sit down. I'm going to grill the steaks while you have a glass or two. Then we'll talk about it."

After consuming two glasses of wine, steak and a crisp salad Ben said, "Thanks for the food. I'm ready to talk now."

"Go ahead," Mae said calmly.

"As you know, my friend Wayne Nichols was the best man at our wedding. He and I have worked together for years and I've learned so much from him. Since he moved in with Lucy, he's also our neighbor. It was because of his help that we solved the murders cases so quickly. I can't imagine asking him to resign," Ben sighed.

"And Dory?" Mae asked.

"It's impossible to even think of the sheriff's office without Dory. When I stepped in as Acting Sheriff, Dory mentored me. Hell, she mothered me! She's been my rock through all these years. If it weren't for her, I'd have handed in my badge and my gun years ago. Asking her to step down would be like firing my own mom." Ben felt his eyes water and angrily brushed the wetness away.

"Why don't you ask Dory and Wayne what they think you should do?" Mae's voice was calm. "They might surprise you. Wayne mentioned once that he'd been thinking of changing directions—doing something other than working homicides. Most of his career has been spent trying to get justice for the dead, and Dory might want to retire. She is certainly well past retirement age."

"Hah! If she ever told anyone her age, it's not on any paperwork in my office. She'd murder me, or file an age-discrimination lawsuit, if I even hinted that I was letting her go because of her age."

"I'm sorry, Ben. This is just a tough situation. I assume you could keep both of them if you terminated Mrs. Coffin and both deputies, or Hadley and Emma, right?"

"The lab techs?" Ben shook his head. "No. We need them. And we could use more deputies, not less. Rob's right, we're top-heavy."

"Then please consider asking Wayne and Dory what they think you should do. Both of them have always put the needs of the office first. Now you, my handsome husband, are going to do the dishes while I get ready for bed. Sorry, but I've got to lie down. I've been having Braxton-Hicks all afternoon."

"What the hell are Braxton-Hicks?" Ben's anxiety about Mae's pregnancy ratcheted up once again.

"False labor," Mae patted her stomach and winced. "I keep telling myself, it'll all be worth it in the end. Even if I make it to full term, it's only about six weeks away."

Ben gave her a half-hearted smile and got up to clear the table.

BEN ASKED DORY TO COME into his office the following morning. He dreaded what he was about to say, but after spending the whole night going over the reduced budget, he knew he had few options. Dory breezed in wearing orange capris, a striped orange T-shirt, black high-top Converse shoes and a baseball cap with a turkey pin that said, "Gobble gobble." He suppressed a grin and shook his head.

"What's up, boss man?" Dory asked as she plopped down into the chair in front of Ben's desk.

"As you predicted, we took a horrendous hit on the budget last night. I was prepared to fight the Commissioner all the way, but Rob made me see sense. The truth is that most of our budget is in personnel and the office needs more help, not less. We don't even have a dedicated drug unit and our IT is laughable. Dory, this is just about killing me, but I wonder if you have any ideas?" Ben could hardly meet her eyes. It was quiet in the old office as Dory pondered the implications of his words. When Ben finally got up the courage to raise his eyes, there was an expression of sad determination on Dory's face.

"Are you asking me to retire, Ben Bradley?"

"No, I'm not, but …

"I know it would help. My salary is the highest in the office. You could hire two more deputies and have money left over without me. My pension is fully vested, and pensions aren't paid out of your budget," she mused.

"Why don't you take some time to think about it? Maybe we can come up with another option."

"No, I don't need any more time, I'll do it. I have no idea what I'll do with myself, but I'll come up with something," she leaned back with a sigh.

"I don't want you to leave the office until after the first of the year. I need time to figure out how to run things around here without your help," Ben looked at her imploringly.

"What about me staying on part-time until Christmas, and then being on-call after that for a few months?"

"That's a good idea, Dory, but only if you agree to continue to boss me around from time to time. I'd also like your input on any new hires. Staff meetings just won't be the same without you. You're welcome any time you want to join us you know."

"You got it." Dory stood up to leave. It was obvious she was trying to look nonchalant, but she was blinking back tears. "Do you want to see Wayne this morning, too?" she asked. "I better not be the only person on the chopping board, Sheriff," she tilted her head at her boss with narrowed eyes.

"You're not." Ben said, grimly. "He's next."

An hour later, Chief Detective Wayne Nichols entered Ben's office. Ben noticed he looked slimmer and had a new haircut. Living with his girlfriend Lucy, an ER physician at Rosedale General, was having a positive impact.

"Good morning, my friend," Ben said and rose to shake Wayne's hand. "Have a seat."

"How's Mae?" Wayne asked. "Not that I'm asking for any

medical details, mind you, but Lucy said she'd kill me if I didn't at least ask."

"She's having false labor pains." Ben took a shaky breath. "I can't quite remember the two-word phrase she used but the words started with a B and an H."

"Like Bounty Hunter?" Wayne asked. "Bank Heist? Battery and Homicide?"

"You definitely think like a cop, Wayne," Ben laughed "The doctor told her she has to take it easy. The longer the twins stay in-utero the better for them. She's closed the kennel for the duration."

"Probably a good idea," Wayne said. "No need for more small talk. I already know why I'm here. Dory called me. She said she's agreed to be on call after the first of the year due to the budget cut. The woman has always been a good soldier." Ben knew it was the highest compliment Wayne could have paid her. "I'm prepared to follow orders as well, if you're about to ask me to step down," Wayne's voice was gruff.

"God no. I don't want either of you to go, but the office is understaffed at the lower levels. We need a dedicated drug officer among other things. Would you want to take that on?"

"Hell no. I hate what drugs do to people, and the truth is I'm ready for a change."

"I dread thinking about what would happen if there was another murder in Rose County. Our closure rate is among the best in the nation. I'm afraid I'd never catch the killer if you weren't my partner," Ben sighed. "I need you here full-time until the first of the year and to be a consultant after that. Would that work for you?"

"Let's say just for major crimes. That's my forte. It's a wrench thinking of not working together, but the needs of the county and its citizens must prevail. Do you still want to have coffee at the Donut Den on Monday mornings?"

"I can't give that up," Ben bit his lip, trying not to take it all back and ask him to stay.

"Guess that's it then," Wayne got to his feet and saluted his commanding officer.

Ben immediately stood and returned Wayne's salute, trying and failing to contain a flood of profound regret.

# THREE

IT WAS COLD AND RAINY on Friday afternoon when Tammy West, who was carrying her six-week-old son Troy in his car seat, steered her older son away from a puddle and towards her best friend's doorway. At seventeen months, young Noah Bennet (nicknamed NB) was happy to stay out in the rain indefinitely, but Tammy lured him up the steps by telling him he could ring the doorbell. Mae opened the door with a smile on her face. *Wow, that belly's gotten big*, Tammy thought.

"Umm-Ah," NB said, in answer to Mae's greeting. "Umm-Ah."

"That's my son's pathetic attempt to say 'Mama.' Noah Bennet West, you just come in the house right now." Her toddler had headed back toward a puddle, but his mother managed to grab him by his red raincoat and get all three of them in the house. She handed the sleeping infant in his car seat to Mae.

"So, it's Noah Bennett now?" her very pregnant friend asked. Mae walked into the kitchen and placed Troy's car seat on the counter, poured a cup of coffee for Tammy and put goldfish crackers on a plastic plate for the toddler. "What happened to calling him NB?"

Tammy hung her coat and Noah's raincoat on the hooks in

the back hall of Mae's farmhouse, pulled off her son's muddy red boots and held out her hand for the coffee. "He gets to be NB when he behaves. Stomping in rain puddles gets him the full moniker. He can clearly say Dada but not Mama. Very irritating. Why did he have to learn to run so early? I used to call him my 'suitcase baby' because I could put him somewhere and he would stay put. I'm sure I was never such a handful for my mama." She frowned at the back of her adorable curly-headed son, running unsteadily down the hall to release Mae's dogs from the laundry room.

"Puh-leeze!" Mae said. "I clearly remember a time in the fourth grade when we were walking home from school in the rain and you actually laid down in a puddle right in front of your house. You kept saying that the rain was so warm, and you just had to feel it. I was afraid your mother was going to skin you alive!"

"Funny," Tammy grinned. "I have no memory of any such thing. Come here, you, and give me a hug. I've hardly seen you lately."

The two friends hugged awkwardly around Mae's big belly, as four dogs hurtled into the kitchen pursued by a giggling toddler. Titan the older corgi, Tallulah the black pug, young corgi Tatie and basset hound Cupcake all sat obediently in front of Mae's bottom kitchen drawer—the one they knew contained the dog treats.

"Meee do," NB said and pulled open the drawer. Mae knelt down to help him dispense the treats. Having finished his favorite activity, NB grabbed a handful of goldfish crackers and toddled out of the kitchen pursued by the four dogs.

"So, what's happening at the sheriff's office? My mother said the news is all around Birdy's Salon that your handsome husband has fired Wayne Nichols."

"Your mom's salon has always been the best place to pick up gossip," Mae smiled.

"It certainly is. It's been rumor central ever since Gramma Birdy opened the place in nineteen fifty-two and that didn't change when Mama took over. She said Dory Clarkson's out too. I can't believe it. Miss Dory's a fixture at the sheriff's office."

"Well, let me correct some of the gossip. Ben called me after he talked to them this morning. Dory and Wayne are both voluntarily retiring from the office. Nobody was fired. In fact, Ben tried to get Wayne to head up the new Drug Education Unit they need. Wayne was the one who declined. He'll stay on-call for major crimes and Ben will still have coffee with him every Monday morning at the Donut Den. At Ben's request, Dory is working part-time and attending staff meetings to keep tabs on everyone and help interview the applicants for the new positions. It was all very amicable. There's going to be a joint Christmas and going-away party for them both in a couple of weeks. Hope I'm still pregnant then."

"Really, you still want to be pregnant then?"

"You know all babies do better later in life if they achieve a normal birth weight. My doctor says he wants both twins to weigh at least four pounds."

"Well, I'm delighted I'm not pregnant," Tammy said. "It's going to be harder this time to get my figure back, they say the more children you have the harder it is, but I've started exercising. How's the dog boarding business?"

"I've had to shut the kennel down. The doctor said I have to take it easy or he'll put me on bed-rest. When I start up again, I've decided to change direction. I'm going to continue to board dogs, but I'm not going to breed puppies ever again. There are just too many unwanted dogs in our community. I can't bear the thought that one of the puppies from my kennel might end up in a shelter. That way I'll have more time for painting."

Tammy eyed Mae's burgeoning stomach doubtfully. "You should probably ask your sister about how much time you're going to have for anything but your babies after they're born. Speaking of the twins, are you going to find out if you're having boys or girls?"

"No, I want to be surprised."

"This one is my last, I swear," Tammy smiled at her infant sleeping peacefully in his seat on the counter.

"I don't believe it. I always pictured you with a big family—walking five kids to the bus stop," Mae said as Tammy gave her an evil glare.

"If you weren't pregnant, I'd happily strangle you, Mae Bradley," she said.

"Whatever. How's business with Local Love?" Mae asked. Local Love was Tammy's match-making service which had been a surprising success in small town Rosedale. It had been Tammy's unrelenting efforts to get her best friend to sign-up with Local Love, along with a murder in Mae's neighborhood that had initially brought Mae and Ben together.

"Rob Fuller, that cute detective who works for Ben, has actually signed up. He had his eyes on Deputy Cam before he discovered that she bats for the other team. Just about killed him to find out she was in a committed relationship—with a girlfriend."

"Rob makes puppy dog eyes at every unattached woman who comes into his orbit. If ever a guy needed a girlfriend, it's Rob."

"I've got a new software package that matches people based on the answers they give to my questions. I review their answers before I forward the matches to the client. Some people lie on their applications, you know. Remember Rosie Lawler?"

"She graduated with us, didn't she?"

"She sure did and put her age down as twenty-five. She's thirty-one if she's a day. And she used her high school graduation picture. Idiot. As if I'd be fooled by that. I called her up and told her to correct the information or I'd dump her as a Local Love client."

"Have you found anyone for Rob yet? Anyone honest, that is," Mae said. "I remember Rosie trying to copy off my math tests in middle school."

"That's hilarious. Math was your worst subject. Rosie should've known better," Tammy snickered.

Mae frowned at her best friend. "Have you found anyone for Rob?"

"What with a newborn and an obstreperous toddler, I haven't had time. I will though. You know me. I hate to see any bachelor stay that way. Men need guidance. They get into all sorts of trouble without a woman keeping them in line.I always look at whether there would be chemistry between the couple. As you can tell from the short interval between my pregnancies, there's plenty of chemistry between me and Patrick. You must have gotten pregnant on your honeymoon, so I'm guessing there's no lack of sparks in your marriage either."

Mae giggled. "Tammy, you crack me up."

# FOUR

———

D ARK CLOUDS COVERED the November sky when Ben got out of his truck in the parking lot of the sheriff's office early Monday morning. A large German Shepherd with a dangling leash ran up to him barking loudly.

"Come over here, boy," Ben called, patting his thigh. The dog moved about ten feet closer and stopped, still barking. Ben approached the dog, trying to step on his leash to trap him, but the dog eluded him and moved further away. When it happened a third time, Ben asked, "Are you trying to tell me something, buddy?"

The dog turned and ran down to the corner of Columbia Street, the entrance to a neighborhood of small well-kept houses. Ben pursued. Hearing the dog bark, a young man stepped out onto his porch and Ben stopped to ask him if he knew the dog.

"That's old lady Cooper's dog, his name is Emmet. Usually very well behaved. Plus, she has an invisible fence, but it looks like her dog's wearing his regular collar now."

"Thanks. Do you know where she lives?"

"Four houses down on this side of the street."

Ben trotted toward the dog who had stopped on the sidewalk in front of the house.

"Emmet, come here," he called, just as he noticed an older

woman lying in the grass at the foot of the porch steps. Ben rushed over and knelt beside her. There was an oxygen tank lying on its side several feet from her. The nasal tube was disconnected. Ben tried her pulse but could feel nothing. He leaned his ear down close to the woman's mouth and could tell she was breathing, but faintly. Reluctant to administer CPR when he knew what could go wrong if he made a mistake, he pulled the tank over and inserted the oxygen tube into the woman's nose. Her breathing seemed stronger afterwards, but she was still unconscious.

"Mrs. Cooper, can you hear me?" Ben asked the woman, reaching for his cell phone to call 911. When the dispatcher picked up, he said, "This is Sheriff Bradley, I need an ambulance at forty-five forty Columbia. Forthwith. Victim is Mrs. Cooper, unconscious elderly woman."

"On the way, Sheriff," the dispatcher said.

While he waited for the ambulance, Ben grabbed Emmet's leash and led him up on the porch. The dog's invisible fence collar was lying in his dog bed. Mrs. Cooper must have removed it and put the dog's regular collar and leash on before setting off on their walk. She wouldn't have wanted to shock her pet as they left the property.

"Emmet, come here."

Ben removed the dog's regular collar and leash, and put the invisible fence collar back on. It would prevent the dog from leaving the property. "Okay, Emmet, you can go now," he said, and the dog walked to his mistress and laid down, his eyes never leaving her face.

Just then the ambulance pulled up and cut its lights and siren.

"Good morning, Sheriff Bradley," one of the paramedics said. "We'll take it from here." He checked the patient, getting vitals and making sure the woman's oxygen was connected securely. A second paramedic unloaded a wheeled gurney and together the two men loaded Mrs. Cooper into the ambulance.

"What will happen to the dog?" Ben asked the EMT.

"We'll call Animal Control. They'll come get him. Okay?"

Ben hesitated and then said, "No, I'd rather leave him here for now. He's got an invisible fence and won't get out again. I'll get someone to take care of him. He's not going to want to be very far from the house in hopes that his owner returns. I'm impressed that he went to find help."

"That's one smart dog," the EMT said in admiration.

Having obtained a promise to get a call from the hospital updating him on Mrs. Cooper's condition, Ben watched the ambulance depart for Rosedale General with lights and siren back on. He walked up the stairs to the covered porch. The front door was unlocked, and he found and filled bowls of water and food, leaving them on the porch for Emmet, right beside his oversized dog bed. He checked under the doormat, found the inevitable key and locked the door behind him.

"You stay here Emmet. Stay," Ben ordered, and the dog returned to the area of the lawn where only minutes earlier Mrs. Cooper lay. "Good dog." Ben patted him on the head and walked back to the office.

Sophie Coffin, the office manager, was on the phone when he arrived. Unlike Dory, she was always professionally dressed. This morning she was wearing navy slacks and a gray cardigan over a white blouse. She ended the call and smiled at her boss. "Good morning, Sheriff, who was in the ambulance that just raced by, do you know?"

"It was a Mrs. Cooper who lives on Columbia."

Sophie's face fell into a worried frown. "Her first name is Myra. She's a friend of my mother-in-law's. What happened?"

"She apparently slipped and fell. When I got there, she was lying in the grass. Her dog, Emmet, came over here for help. The hospital's going to call with an update on her condition soon. Can you be sure I get the message? I need to know her next of kin." Seeing her expression, he added, "I'm not saying she's going to die, but I want to inform her family that she's in the hospital, and someone needs to take care of the dog until she's back at home."

"You got it," she answered, handing him a piece of paper with the day's appointments neatly typed on it. "Didn't want you to forget that you have several applicants for the new positions coming in this morning. Miss Dory's going to assist. Anything else?"

Ben didn't answer her question for a moment. He was deep in thought.

"Sheriff, did you hear me?"

Ben roused himself and said, "Yes, there's something else. I want George to go over to Mrs. Cooper's place. Tell him I said to put yellow crime scene tape around her house ASAP."

"You think a crime might have been committed?" Sophie Coffin's eyebrows rose above her glasses.

"I'm probably overreacting, but I don't want anybody in that house until we have time to check it out thoroughly. Get George moving." Mrs. Coffin pressed the intercom calling, "Deputy George Phelps. Come to the front desk immediately."

Going down the hall to his office, Ben saw someone walking away from him toward the jail. Thinking it was his deputy, he called, "George, come here a minute." The person turned around and Ben felt his stomach fall. It wasn't George, it was Miss Dory Clarkson. In a brown pantsuit, the exact color of the Sheriff's Department uniforms. *Oh man, I'm gonna be in trouble.*

"Did you actually mistake my sylph-like figure for Deputy George's pudgy body?" Dory glared at Ben with steely eyes. "Do you want to live long enough to attend the birth of your twins? If so, you will apologize immediately and abjectly."

"Dory, I'm so sorry. The fluorescent bulb was flickering and all I saw was pants and a jacket."

Dory's eyes were still narrowed.

"Seriously. You are a truly gorgeous woman and how I could have mistaken you for George…. I'm an idiot, obviously. I'm so sorry."

"Well, I'm not quite ready to accept your apology, Sheriff.

More punishment is probably in order." Her voice was stern, but a little grin pulled at the corner of her mouth.

"Truce?" Ben held out his hand. "We have interviews to do today you know."

"Truce," Dory said as they shook hands.

Several hours later, two of the candidates who had applied to head up the new Rosedale Drug Education & Prevention office (DEP) had come and gone. Dory and Ben were commiserating.

"I can't imagine how those two wet-behind-the-ears cops thought they were qualified to head up a drug prevention office," Ben said. "How come you didn't sort them out before they got to the interview stage?"

"The problem is the salary, Sheriff. Both of those guys had worked for big city police posts and had salaries close to or even above what we're offering. They weren't likely to take on more responsibility for the same or less money, and we only had three applicants for the position," Dory said.

"I know," Ben was gloomy. "What's the deal with the last guy?"

"I have hopes for him. He's older, in his late forties. He's married with three sons and I've heard that his wife has connections in Rosedale. The boys are in middle and high school and they probably want a good school district. I think he might be our guy. His name is Derek Harvey. He comes to us from Narcotics in Nashville."

"Let's have him then."

When Mrs. Coffin knocked on his door minutes later with the candidate, Ben stood to shake hands with the tall dark-haired man. He liked his grip. Strong without being bone-crushing. "Have a seat, Derek. This is Dory Clarkson. Miss Clarkson's an Investigator in my office. We're going to be doing the interview together."

"Glad to meet you, Miss Clarkson. I've heard about you. You have street cred all the way to Nashville—juice, as they say." he smiled, and Dory beamed.

After running through the standard set of questions, Ben asked the candidate why he wanted to change jobs.

"I've worked narcotics most of my career and feel I'm ready to head up a DEP Unit. I want to concentrate on education and plan to form partnerships with physicians, clinics and pharmacists who have been way too generous in handing out pain killing drugs like Oxy—especially to kids. Since heroin is cheaper, users are turning to it with often fatal results."

"What's your family situation?" Ben asked. "I know narcotics and especially undercover can wreak hell on a marriage. Does your wife have anything to do with you wanting to change careers?"

"She sure does. Her parents live on a farm near Rosedale and she wants to be closer to them as they get older, and she wants a suburban school for our sons. We're tired of big city living and I'm burned out on undercover. I'm aware that the salary might be a little lower than I've been getting, but starting a new DEP unit will be worth it. I do have a question though."

"Go ahead."

"I got to thinking that the problem in schools is both drugs and guns and wondered if you would consider combining both drug and firearm education into one unit. I'd be interested in heading that."

"Now that's a really good idea," Dory said. She glanced at Ben, giving him an infinitesimal nod. Ben got the message.

"It's going to be good working with you, Derek. Assuming your references check out, the job is yours. You'll start after Thanksgiving." Ben watched a delighted grin spread across the man's face.

"I'll tell my wife we can start house hunting," Derek replied.

At a quick knock on the door, Ben called, "Come in."

Sophie Coffin handed him a slip of paper. "Excuse me for interrupting, Sir, but you wanted the info on Mrs. Cooper as soon as it came in." She swallowed and looked down at the message in Ben's hand. "They say she's likely."

At the word, both Derek and Dory looked grave. The word "likely" was police vernacular meaning likely to die. Turning back to Derek Harvey, Ben said, "Dory can give you the particulars on salary and benefits. I have to get to the hospital."

# FIVE

⁓

**D**ORY CLARKSON, Sheriff's Office Investigator, had just walked into her house in the Flowerpot District, feeling low and unneeded when her cellphone rang. Removing it from her purse, she saw Ben Bradley's picture on the screen and pressed the talk button.

"Hello."

"Dory, I'm still here at the hospital. I have bad news. Mrs. Cooper never recovered consciousness and she's in the morgue. I need your help."

"I'm sorry to hear that, Sheriff," Dory sighed. "But you seem to have forgotten that I tendered, and you accepted my offer of resignation on Friday. I'm on limited part-time status until Christmas and I already assisted in the hiring of a new employee this morning." There was silence on the other end of the call. Letting the stillness hang in the air for several seconds, Dory finally took pity on her boss. "So, what did you need?"

"I want to get an autopsy done on Mrs. Cooper. I went down to the morgue and when I saw her body, I got that uneasy feeling…"

All members of the cop fraternity knew to pay attention to that prickly feeling and Ben's intuition in these matters was almost invariably right. There had been a couple of times he'd been spectacularly wrong, however, and Dory thought this was one of them.

"You think that Mrs. Cooper's death was murder? Boss, you're nuts. A seventy-something old lady who's on oxygen takes a tumble down her front stairs, her oxygen tube is dislodged, and you think she was done in? No way."

"I know it seems ridiculous, but I do," Ben insisted. "I want Dr. Estes to do an autopsy to confirm my hunch, but he won't do it. Says I need her next of kin to authorize it and that it's a waste of his time and talents. I asked Mrs. Coffin to find Mrs. Cooper's family earlier. Can you find out if she was able to locate anyone? I also need to find out if the victim had a lawyer, and we need to make a plan to take care of her dog. His name is Emmet."

Dory felt a tiny quiver of delight. Of course, the old woman's death was sad, but it was gratifying to know they couldn't get along without her at the office. "I guess, I can manage to help you out, just don't make a habit of it. Just kidding, I'm on it," she ended the call.

After letting out her own dog, True, for a quick potty break, Dory drove back to the sheriff's office, parked her car and walked down the street to Mrs. Cooper's house. The woman's dog was on duty and ran up barking. He didn't cross the invisible fence though, just stayed at the edge of the property guarding his territory. "Good boy, Emmet," she said, and the dog settled.

Two houses further down the street, Dory hit pay dirt. A stout white woman was sweeping her porch and front stairs, peering at the surrounding houses all the while. Clearly the neighborhood snoop, she stopped working the minute she spotted Dory.

"I wonder if I could trouble you for some information, ma'am. I'm an Investigator with the sheriff's office and I need to ask you some questions about your neighbor, Mrs. Cooper."

"Certainly," the woman bustled importantly down the sidewalk. She held her hand out to shake with Dory. "I'm Effie

Martin, the Neighborhood Watch officer."

There's a shocker. "If you're not too busy, Mrs. Martin, could I come inside for a few minutes?" Dory pulled out her identification which the woman looked at carefully.

"It's Miss Martin, not Mrs.," she said in a prissy voice. "Since you're with the police, however, I feel I must do my civic duty. Please come in."

Dory suppressed a grin and followed Miss Martin into her bungalow. It had been built in the thirties and while outdated it was immaculate—right down to the white doily antimacassars on the backs of the chairs. Their purpose was to keep hair products from staining the upholstery. They were so out-of-date, Dory's grandmother was the last person she could remember using them.

"Would you like a cup of tea?" Miss Martin asked.

"Yes, thank you," Dory replied. A large yellow tomcat walked leisurely into the room and jumped up on the wide window sill. He fixed his green eyes on a goldfinch outside in a tree and then moved his gaze to the street. *Miss Martin's assistant, no doubt.* After puttering around in the kitchen for several minutes, Effie Martin came back into the living room with a tray and two steaming mugs of tea. She placed the tray on the coffee table and turned an expectant face to Dory.

"I'm looking for some information about your neighbor, Mrs. Cooper," Dory paused to look carefully at the woman's face. She wondered if the two women had been friends and was prepared to offer sincere condolences. However, Miss Martin's eyes narrowed at hearing Mrs. Cooper's name. The two were definitely not friends. "I'm sorry to tell you that Mrs. Cooper passed away this morning at Rosedale General," Dory continued.

"I see," Effie said, primly. "I heard the siren on the ambulance and walked down toward her house immediately. I saw the sheriff and the emergency services workers in the yard loading her in the ambulance. It's my job to keep the neighbors properly informed, so I called the hospital. Since

I'm not a relative they wouldn't tell me anything, but I'm not surprised to learn that she died. The woman was at least a decade older than me, and she was on oxygen. She'd been a lifetime smoker. It was the height of stupidity to acquire that dog of hers. Large German Shepherds, especially young males, are far too obstreperous for elderly woman to manage. I told her at the time that a cat would…"

Dory interrupted, not wanting to hear the whole dog vs. cat argument. "I don't suppose you have any idea whether Mrs. Cooper had children, do you?"

"I do. She had an only son, a good-for-nothing who couldn't hold a job. He passed away about five years ago. I always suspected drugs. Edward was his name."

"Did Edward marry? Have any children himself?"

"There was a marriage, lasted only a few years, and I heard there was a daughter named Carol Anne, if I'm remembering correctly. Never met her. I think she would be in her early twenties by now. She will likely inherit, although if that girl ever came to visit her grandmother it's news to me. I'm curious to know what else you can share with me. If you need to have me keep things confidential, I promise to do that." She leaned forward, intent on dragging every bit of news she could get out of Dory.

Dory knew full well that whatever she told Miss Martin would be all around the neighborhood in minutes. It was time to distract the snoop with flattery and Dory poured it on. "You're amazing, Miss Martin. I can't believe you knew all that. The neighborhood is lucky to have someone like you to be their Neighborhood Watch officer. If more people had your sense of civic duty, our jobs would be far easier. I know you're busy, but do you think you could possibly answer one or two more questions? I promise I won't keep you long."

"Certainly," Miss Martin preened a little, "Would you like a cookie? I have some I just took out of the oven. Chocolate chip."

Several more cups of tea and multiple cookies later, Dory

had obtained the name of Mrs. Cooper's lawyer. It was her good friend Evangeline Bon Temps, a Rosedale attorney who had helped the sheriff's office in the past.[2]

"I know Ms. Bon Temps well," Dory said. "One other question before I let you go; I assume Mrs. Cooper owned her home?"

"She's lived here for years, so I thought it would be paid for, but I recently learned that Mrs. Cooper still rented her home."

"That's interesting," Dory said.

"Mr. Pierce Turner, a property developer who is no better than a common thug, owns her house and all but a couple of the other houses on the street. He started buying them up several years ago, probably bought Mrs. Cooper's from her old landlord. I had the good sense to purchase my house outright. It's paid for and worth a bundle."

Dory suppressed her inclination to tell the woman to stop patting herself on the back, saying, "I noticed several homes on the street have been torn down. What's going on?"

"A Nashville builder has recently started working in Rosedale. He's known for creating upscale homes. The residents on the block who own their homes have been approached and offered money to sell. I'm going to earn a very good return on my investment. I've put in an offer on a nice condo on the edge of town. The complex allows cats, although not dogs," Miss Martin said, sanctimoniously.

After a few more probing questions and thickly laid on blandishments, Dory learned that the 'thug-like' Pierce Turner was a partner in the building venture with a Mr. Scott Luttrell.

"I wonder if you could tell me why you called Mr. Turner a thug, Miss Martin?" Dory asked.

"Well, he dresses nicely, I'll give him that. He always wears expensive suits and ties. People around here are afraid to cross him. That's why all the residents are leaving. The man's also known as a cheapskate. I was the only one on the street who stood up to him—he's agreed to pay full market value for my

2  Farrell, Lia, Two Dogs Lie Sleeping, Camel Press, 2014

house. Plus, Pierce and his so-called assistant, Dante Jones, have been telling people they need to move out before their leases are up."

"You're right, Miss Martin. That sounds about as shady as can be."

WALKING BACK DOWN THE SIDEWALK, Dory thought about the Sheriff's sense that Mrs. Cooper had been murdered. In order to prove a case of murder, they always needed the big three: Means, Motive and Opportunity. If Mrs. Cooper died due to foul play, Dory was pretty sure she had just found a solid motive. To turn the neighborhood into an upscale expensive one, Luttrell and Pierce needed all the residents on the street to evacuate their houses. Opportunity would also be easy to prove as it was likely that Mr. Pierce Turner was in the area frequently. His appearance wouldn't raise a single eyebrow, not even those of Miss Neighborhood Watch. Now all they needed was the means, the murder weapon. That might be a lot harder to come by.

# SIX

⁓

SUZANNE DECEMBER HAD LONG MADE it a policy never to knock on her daughter's doors when she arrived at their homes, even early in the day. It kept her girls on their toes, although occasionally she did spot dirty dishes or overhear an argument. When she arrived at Mae's house the Tuesday before Thanksgiving and walked into the farmhouse kitchen, however, she was greeted with muffled sobs. Her daughter, Mae, was sitting at the kitchen table with her head down on her arms.

"Oh, Sweetheart, what is it?"

Still wearing her maternity pajamas, Mae raised her head. She was a bit startled at the appearance of her mother in her kitchen but tried vainly to smile. "Good morning, Mama," she said.

"What's wrong, Honey?"

"Being pregnant with twins, that's what's wrong," Mae burst into tears again. "I'm just so big! I can't even clean up the kitchen. I was trying to load the dishwasher this morning and bumped the table with my stomach and broke Ben's favorite coffee mug, the one with the sheriff's badge on it. I know all about post-natal depression, but I swear I have pre-natal depression."

"This will all be over soon, sweetie. I remember your sister feeling the same way before the twins were born. Your due date is January third, right? That's just over a month. I promise not to ask you how much weight you've gained," Suzanne grinned impishly.

"You better not," Mae narrowed her eyes. "My stupid doctor told me I can't drive any more. I had an appointment yesterday and he actually laughed when he asked me how I could reach the brakes. I swear I almost slapped the man. He reiterated that I can't even have a glass of wine with dinner and only one cup of coffee a day. I wish I'd gotten a female obstetrician, one who had already had children," she said in disgust.

"You father had the gall to ask me to get on the scale when I was eight months pregnant with you. I damn near had the divorce papers drawn up," Suzanne grinned in remembrance. "Then after you were born my doctor scolded me. You were almost nine pounds and during the delivery apparently, I got a little bit obstreperous. The following morning the doctor came in and said, 'Mrs. December, you bit a nurse last night. You need to apologize to Nurse Wilcox. I said I'd apologize to Louise Wilcox the day she delivered a nine-pound baby," Suzanne told her daughter and Mae managed a watery smile.

"On top of feeling ridiculously huge, Ben and I had an argument this morning and I made him late for work," Mae sounded miserable.

"What was the spat about?"

"Matt was here, I was trying to get him ready for school and I finally got down on the floor to tie his shoes and then I couldn't get back up again. I told Ben he had to take him to school and to inform Katie that Matt couldn't come back until after the babies were born. He was supposed to be with us for Thanksgiving and go back to Katie's the following Monday, but I just can't do it. Matt started to cry, and Ben said he was working a case and he didn't have time to drop him by the school. I told him he didn't have a choice and then Matt said he hated me being pregnant," Mae started to tear up again.

"Sounds about par for the course to me," Suzanne said in

a calm tone.

"Matt also said he was his father's only child and he wanted things to stay that way."

"Well, it's a little late for that now. He'll adjust. As I recall, July wasn't thrilled when I got pregnant with you either. One time when you were about eight months old and crawling, you knocked down a tower she was building with blocks. She picked you up and put you in your playpen and told me to take you back to the hospital," Suzanne shook her head. "I'd say Matt's reaction is pretty normal."

"I guess," Mae sniffled.

"So, changing the subject, we've had a talk in the family. We think you're going to need to have someone here during the day until the babies are born. Your father, sister and I are going to take turns coming by each day. We can do errands for you, bring food over and take you to your appointments. If Ben is out late chasing a bad guy, we'll stay over." Suzanne looked at her daughter to see if she would be okay with the plan. Mae clambered out of her chair and hugged her mother tightly.

"That will be wonderful, Mama. Are you sure? If you're over here, who's going to keep an eye on your dogs?" Suzanne and her husband, Don, had a pair of Jack Russell terriers named Lil'bit and Kudzu who still needed constant supervision, despite being well beyond puppyhood.

"As you know, those dogs were your father's idea, not mine," Suzanne said, unfazed at the thought of what the dogs might destroy in her beautiful home. "Your father just needs to man up and watch them while I'm gone. The problem is that he's too lenient. Whenever he has anything to eat, he shares his food with them. Lil'bit is getting fat. If I'm not there, maybe all three of them will get out of the house to take some walks. A bit of exercise wouldn't hurt your father either,"

"Are you staying with me today?" Mae asked.

"I am. You just sit there, and I'll finish cleaning up the kitchen. After that, what else needs doing around here?" Suzanne surveyed Mae's house with a gimlet eye. Although it was nearly Thanksgiving, the house lacked any seasonal decorations.

Seeing her mother's face, Mae said, "I don't know if you want to take this on, mama, but I would like a bit of holiday décor put up. Ben got the boxes out of the attic last night, but what with him giving Matt a bath and putting him to bed, none of it was put on the mantle or the dining room table."

"How about I put up what you have and then I'm taking us out to lunch where—in total defiance of your doctor's orders—you are having a glass of wine. When I was pregnant, doctors often encouraged women to have a glass of wine with food during their last trimesters. I had wine with dinner every night and you and July were perfect. Then after lunch we are going to Balsam Hill Nursery. They have the most beautiful wreaths. You go on upstairs now and get dressed."

TWO HOURS LATER SUZANNE AND Mae walked into Balsam Hill Nursery. The owners had done a magnificent job of decorating, managing to hit just the right note that combined a nod to Thanksgiving with an over-the-top Christmas display. They walked over to an entire wall devoted to wreaths.

"These are gorgeous. Look at this one," Mae pointed to a wreath that combined abundant autumn foliage with pine cones and dark green magnolia leaves. "Oh, I like this one too," she indicated an olive branch wreath with acorns.

"Pick out the two you like best, one for your front door and one for above the fireplace," Suzanne said smiling. "My treat. I'm going to check out the Christmas tree section."

Mae and Ben had announced several weeks earlier they were going to take his son to a local Christmas tree farm to cut down a tree. While Suzanne appreciated the beauty of real trees at Christmas, this year it just wasn't going to work. Mae wasn't up to riding in a wagon bouncing across a Christmas tree farm and the pine needles on the floors afterwards would be a nightmare to clean up while taking care of twins. Suzanne quickly found an artificial Vermont White Spruce that was pre-lit and astoundingly realistic. Beside the tree display there was a shelf with bottles of pine-scented spray. She tried it and it smelled wonderful. By the time Mae had picked out her wreaths, Suzanne had purchased the tree and one of the young male employees was loading it into the back of her van. She went back inside to purchase Mae's wreath selections.

When they arrived back at Mae's farmhouse and the wreaths were hung, Suzanne told Mae it was time for her to take a nap. Mae gratefully acceded. She waddled upstairs and plopped down on her bed. Suzanne pulled off her daughter's shoes and when she laid back on the pillows, pulled a blanket gently up to her chin.

Walking back downstairs and outside, Suzanne managed to get the large box containing the pre-lit tree into the house. A bit out of breath, she sat down and checked the time. It was five-thirty. She called the sheriff's office. When Dory answered, Suzanne asked her why she was on phones. "I thought you just retired."

"They're having a hard time adjusting plus Sophie took some vacation time this week," Dory replied, and Suzanne could hear the amusement in her voice.

"Tell Sheriff Bradley it's his mother-in-law and she wants a word with him now," she said in her coolest tone.

"It's about time somebody reined him in," Dory's voice was cheerful. "Hang on."

Ben's subsequent "Hello" sounded a bit rattled.

"Ben, this is Suzanne, and we need to talk," she heard a sound resembling a gulp. Good. "First of all, I don't care what case you're pursuing, you will be home by six every single night until the babies are born." There was a brief silence before she continued. "Furthermore, you will be doing all the cooking, dishes, laundry and housework during that period. Your son, Matt, will not be coming back to sleep over until after the babies are born. He can visit for short periods as long as you are present. I have purchased an artificial Christmas tree. It's in its packaging to the left of the fireplace. You need to leave the office, and have it set up by the time Mae gets up from her nap. Is that clear?"

After a brief hesitation, Ben said, "Yes ma'am. Crystal clear. I'm leaving for home now. I'll see you soon."

"Oh yes you will, Ben Bradley, you definitely will," she muttered.

Feeling a glow of accomplishment, Suzanne walked out of the house, locking the door behind her. She had left a list of things for her husband, Don, to do in her absence. It was time to see what the man had accomplished.

# SEVEN

———

JULIA GRACE POWELL had been given the nickname July as a toddler. The switch from Julia to July came about when she couldn't say the name Maeve and started calling her little sister Mae. With birthdays in May and July, it was inevitable that the girls became known as Mae and July. With December for a last name, they were teased unmercifully about their "calendar" names until both girls married. They were now July Powell and Mae Bradley and both were relieved to have the stale jokes about their names over and done with.

July arrived at her parents' house in the early afternoon of Thanksgiving Day with her husband Fred, twin sons Nate and Parker and daughter Olivia. She and her mother had worked out the menu and July's contributions earlier in the week. Mae wanted to cook something too, but both her mother and sister flatly refused.

"Boys, get back here," Fred called as his sons raced toward the front door. "Don't just run into the house. You need to help with some of this food. Your mother will tell you what to carry."

"Nate, you take the sweet potato casserole. Parker, you carry the green bean casserole. Livi you can carry something, too. Here's the apple pie. Fred, you take the wine," July smiled approvingly at her family as they lined up single-file on the sidewalk to take the food inside. She grabbed the broccoli salad, a bouquet of purple mums and they trekked in. It was sunny and warm, but cooler weather was expected to move in later in the day.

July's mother, Suzanne, was standing in the open doorway smiling at the family, taking coats and giving out hugs. "Don, tear yourself away from the football game and give me a hand out here," she called, and Don December appeared to welcome the family.

July turned her head at the sound of her brother-in-law Ben's truck in the driveway. He and her sister Mae had arrived. When Mae climbed out of the truck, Livi called out, "Mom, Aunt Mae is wearing slippers and pajamas! You said I had to dress up!"

"Hush honey, your Aunt Mae isn't feeling well," July said quietly, noticing Mae's despairing expression.

"I couldn't get my stupid fat feet in my shoes today," Mae whispered to July who nodded in understanding. She herself had once been eight months pregnant with twins. The whole group came inside the house and Mae's father helped his youngest daughter into his recliner. He pulled the lever so Mae's feet would be raised.

"I thought I got rid of that old thing," July said to her father, frowning at the green plaid monstrosity. July was a designer and had recently remodeled her parents' kitchen, dining and living rooms to make it one large open-concept space. Done in soft grays and white, the old plaid La-Z-Boy didn't exactly fit the design scheme.

"You did, and I've ordered a new one that was acceptable to my wife. She said you would be okay with it too. It's custom leather so it's taking forever to make. In the meantime, Suzanne said I could bring my old La-Z-Boy back into the house. She remembered you sitting in it when you were pregnant for the twins," he smiled, looking at Fred who was handing his sons a football and telling them to stay outside until dinner was ready.

July's father went into the kitchen and began pouring wine for everyone.

"Is Mae allowed to have wine?" July asked Suzanne, frowning at the number of wine glasses.

"Shush," her mother said. "I've decided it's okay for her to have one glass a day since she's so close to the end," she whispered.

"Since when did you become her obstetrician?" July gave her mother a disapproving glance.

"I drank a glass of wine daily throughout both of my pregnancies as soon as I was past the first trimester and you and your sister had perfect APGAR scores. Mae is just so stressed, I thought one glass of wine with food would help." Suzanne turned to Don saying, "Here, bring this little plate of cheese and crackers to Mae to have with her wine."

"Is anyone else coming for dinner today?" July asked, setting her salad on the counter and enjoying the mouth-watering scents of turkey and ham emerging from the oven.

"Ben's parents decided to go to his brother's house when I told them Mae was feeling so poorly. I invited Detective Nichols and his girlfriend, Lucy Ingram, to join us but Wayne volunteered to cover the office today and Lucy said she always worked Thanksgiving at the hospital since so many employees wanted to be at home with their families."

"What about Matt?"

"Katie and her boyfriend decided to take him to Florida to see her parents, they drove down yesterday. Mae and Ben will have him for Thanksgiving next year."

The three men went into the living room to watch football and Suzanne put July's casseroles in the oven to heat. Looking beyond the kitchen island, July thought her mom's dining table looked lovely with a long runner down the center. The design featured pumpkins and vines curling realistically on the fabric. She set her bouquet of mums in the center of the table noticing the soft green placemats with an edging of orange autumn berries. The Thanksgiving dishes and glasses were on the sideboard ready for filling with food. The silverware and napkins were already in place. An hour later, timed perfectly to coincide with half-time for the game, the family assembled at the table.

"Can I say grace?" Livi asked and her grandparents nodded. She quoted, "Thank you God for giving me a home as nice as it can be. Thank you for my family, too. I love them God and I love you."

"Very nice, Livi," July said, and everyone proceeded to dig in as food was passed down the long table. Half an hour later, July looked at her sister who had made a soft noise. "Mae, are you okay?"

"I don't think so," Mae whispered. "I've been having false labor for a week now, but I think this could be the real thing," her eyes looked almost black in her suddenly pale face.

Standing up so quickly that her chair fell over, July announced, "Ben and I are taking Mae to the hospital to see if she's in labor or if it's just another false alarm. Ben, pull the car up."

Over Mae's strongly voiced protests, Ben put on his lights and sirens as they pulled out of her parents' driveway. Cars scooted over to the side of the road to get out of the way. They pulled into the ER loading zone fifteen minutes later and Ben dashed inside returning with a wheelchair and Dr. Lucy Ingram, looking official in her white coat.

"Hello everyone," Lucy said. "Ben, help Mae into the wheelchair and we'll get her inside and have a look. July, come on with us. This little mother-to-be will want her sister and her husband now."

Half an hour later, Lucy had arranged for Mae to be referred on the Obstetrics floor of the hospital. The ER was unusually quiet, due to the Thanksgiving holiday, so Lucy was able to accompany them upstairs to Labor and Delivery. Once there, an ob/gyn resident examined Mae and ordered an ultrasound. Ben followed the orderly who wheeled Mae down the hall for the test.

"HOW ARE YOU FEELING NOW?" July asked, when the orderly brought Mae back from her ultrasound.

"Better, but a little foolish. The pains have stopped, and I'm upset with myself that I interrupted Thanksgiving dinner for nothing," Mae said.

"Better safe than sorry," Ben said, just as the ob/gyn resident reappeared with the results of the ultra-sound. Lucy took a look at them.

"It looks like you'll be staying here overnight at least," Lucy said. "I called your obstetrician and he'll be in tomorrow morning to check on you."

"Could you tell how much the babies weigh by now?" Mae asked the resident.

"One is about three pounds but the other one is just over two. It would be best if we can get you comfortable and not progressing. The longer those two little ones are safe inside, the better," the resident smiled.

"So, there's no chance they would induce her?" July asked. "She's pretty miserable."

"Not my call, but I'd say it's doubtful. Her doctor will decide tomorrow morning," he glanced at Mae who looked like she was going to cry.

"One of us should stay with her," July said, as the white-coated resident nodded and departed.

"I'll stay here tonight," Ben said and reached out his hand for Mae's. "I'll run home to check on the dogs after she falls asleep."

"I'll leave you two alone then and call Fred. He can come pick me up. I'll be back tomorrow morning," July gave her little sister a kiss on the cheek and said goodbye.

She walked out into the hall and called her husband. She was determined to return the next morning to hear what Mae's obstetrician had to say. When Mae heard the resident say he thought it unlikely she would be induced, she had looked so depressed July's heart ached for her.

# EIGHT

———

L UCY LEFT FOR WORK at the hospital before seven the morning after Thanksgiving. She had received a text from Sheriff Ben Bradley late the previous night. Knowing she was able to move mountains inside the hospital bureaucracy, he had asked for her help.

His text read: Could you get Dr. Estes to do an autopsy on Mrs. Cooper? He wants okay from next of kin. Granddaughter Carol Anne Cooper gave verbal approval. I suspect foul play.

Knowing what a stickler Dr. Estes was, Lucy was certain he wouldn't proceed without written approval. Pulling out her cell phone, she called the sheriff's office. Mrs. Coffin, who was at the office early, was able to give her Carol Anne Cooper's phone number.

"Hello," a sleepy voice answered.

"Is this Carol Anne Cooper?" When the sleep-fogged voice made an affirmative sound, Lucy continued. "This is Dr. Ingram calling from Rosedale General Hospital. I understand you spoke with Sheriff Ben Bradley recently and gave verbal permission for an autopsy on your grandmother. Is that correct?"

A long silence followed. Lucy feared that Carol Anne had drifted back into the land of slumber. She raised her voice.

"Miss Cooper, I need your attention. This is official

business."

"Okay, okay," the girl answered.

"What we need is your signature to approve the autopsy on your grandmother. Do you have a fax machine?"

"What? No, I don't," she sounded confused. "Why would I?"

"Is there a UPS store nearby that you could go to?"

"Yes, but they probably aren't open yet. It's pretty early, you know?" She whined.

"Could you go there as soon as they open and call me from the shop? If you tell me their fax number, I'll fax you a paper to sign."

There was another pause.

"Carol Anne, did you hear me? I need you to go to the UPS store as soon as they open and call me from there."

"Fine. I'll call you back."

AN HOUR LATER, HAVING RECEIVED the signed and faxed permission form, Lucy met Sheriff Bradley in the hall just outside the Morgue.

"How was Mae's night?" she asked.

"They gave her something to help her sleep. July's with her now and they're getting her some breakfast. Mae says she feels fine and wants to go home."

"An excellent sign, I would say," Lucy pushed open the swinging door to the morgue. "Good morning, Dr. Estes," she said brightly, as the eminent pathologist who served as Medical Examiner slid a stainless-steel drawer containing a body back into place. Dr. Estes wore glasses and was so tall and thin he resembled a heron. At the moment, a highly irritated heron.

"Seeing you two, I have a feeling my plan for the day just evaporated," Dr. Estes scowled, but he shook hands with Ben and nodded at Lucy. "Do you have written permission for the autopsy yet, Sheriff?"

"Got it right here," Lucy held out the piece of paper.

Dr. Estes grunted and took a long look at the fax. "I don't

have time to do a complete autopsy today, but I will do a visual inspection of the body with you, Sheriff Bradley. Will that suffice for the time being?"

"Yes, that will do," Ben said as Dr. Estes opened the stainless-steel drawer containing Mrs. Cooper's body.

As Dr. Estes began his careful inspection of the naked body, Lucy noted a straight line of bruises across the woman's legs just above her ankles. It looked like a bruise pattern she had once noticed on a patient who came into the ER. That person had tripped over a two-by-four at a construction site.

"I've seen bruises like this before," Lucy began, before being quelled by a fierce glare from the Medical Examiner. Knowing better than to interrupt Dr. Estes' perusal again, Lucy and Ben waited in silence.

"Frankly, I see no signs of untoward injury on this woman's body, Sheriff. She wasn't strangled or asphyxiated. There is no indication of poison and obviously she wasn't shot. I do observe this line of bruises on the front of her lower legs. And a small discoloration on her cheek. See here?" Dr. Estes turned Mrs. Cooper's head and pointed to the scraped area.

"What's your conclusion, doctor?" Lucy asked.

"As you know, Dr. Ingram, I don't provide conclusions until I have done the autopsy, but because of the urgency of the situation, I'm willing to say that the woman tripped over something and fell forwards. She probably bruised her face falling against something hard like a concrete sidewalk."

"She was lying at the foot of her porch steps when I found her," Ben admitted. "Her German Shepherd led me to her. So, you're saying both injuries came from her fall?"

"The facial injury can be easily explained. She must have tripped, fallen forwards and hit her cheek on the sidewalk. I admit I was a bit baffled by the bruises on the front of her lower legs until just now. Since I now know she had a dog, it's obvious the dog pulled his leash across her legs. He may have been chasing something. She probably had him on one of those flexi-leashes, the kind with a long string that rewinds."

Dr. Estes covered the body with a sheet and turned back to Ben saying, "I don't believe there's sufficient evidence here to investigate further, Sheriff. And I understand your wife is soon going to present you with twins, which should keep you plenty busy without imagining crimes where none exist."

"I've seen countless injuries in the ER from patients tripping over that type of leash," Lucy said. "Thank you so much, Dr. Estes."Before Ben could ask any more questions, she hustled him out of the morgue. "So, no cause for alarm then. The patient died from natural causes resulting from a fall. I'd say you could go back upstairs to see Mae…" she trailed off seeing Ben's face. His teeth were clenched. "What is it?"

"That dog wasn't on a flexi-leash, it was a chain-link leash. Mrs. Cooper's line of bruises above her ankles were perfectly straight. They didn't look at all like the marks made by chain links. Someone tripped that poor woman and it caused her death. That kind of crime is always premeditated."

Ben pulled out his phone, turned and started down the hospital hall. Lucy could hear his voice saying, "Wayne, sorry to bother you, my friend, but I need you to go over to Mrs. Cooper's house. Can you make sure George put up the yellow crime scene tape? And that it hasn't been disturbed? Please look for a murder weapon too, something caused our victim to trip. Can you feed and water her dog please? Yes, I know we need to do something about him soon."

LUCY PULLED INTO HER DRIVEWAY around six that evening. It was getting dark, but the porch light was on, and she bit back a curse when she saw her boyfriend Wayne sitting on the front porch. Beside him sat a dog, a very large German Shepherd. She parked her car, got out and slammed the door. She and Wayne had discussed that very dog when they learned Mrs. Cooper had passed away. Lucy had been quite clear. Wayne was not to bring that dog home. They were both working ridiculously long hours. It wouldn't be fair to the animal. Yet here he was. She waited a moment, trying to get her anger under control but then felt her irritation rise even higher when she noticed Wayne feeding the dog a cookie.

"Lordy, Pete," Lucy said in exasperation, walking up to the porch. "Was I not clear, Wayne? We are not going to have a dog. Especially not such a large dog. Take him to the Humane Society now. I'm not having that animal in the house."

"His name is Emmet," Wayne said, giving her an entreating grin. "I googled German dog names and it means universal truth. He's only be here for a little while. We just have to get Mrs. Cooper's granddaughter to come get him. I already called her and left a message. I told her to come to this address and pick him up. I think she'll be here in the morning."

Lucy sighed, knowing she was beaten for the moment. "Well, if it's just for tonight, I guess it will be okay, but the girl sounded flaky to me when I talked to her earlier. I certainly hope she shows up to claim him. Come on, Emmet," she said opening the door to the house. The dog immediately stood and walked over to Lucy. He looked up at her, his tail swishing and his head tilted to one side. She raised her eyebrows. "You sure know how to work a situation, don't you?" When Lucy reached down to pet the dog between his oversized ears. She could swear Emmet was smiling. "Universal truth, my ass," she muttered.

# NINE

───※───

"THAT DOG IS NOT STAYING ALONE in this house all day," Lucy scowled at Wayne. "If you can't get Mrs. Cooper's granddaughter to pick him up this morning, you will be taking the dog to work with you."

Wayne looked down, trying to hide a smile. So far, Carol Anne was a no-show and Emmet had spent the weekend with them. When Wayne had arrived home late Sunday night, he was cold and wet from yet another trip to the victim's house. He snuck into the bedroom quietly, amused to see Lucy sound asleep in their bed with Emmet lying beside right her. His girlfriend was weakening. It was all a front, she actually liked the dog.

"I'll take him with me, no problem," Wayne said giving Lucy a kiss before heading out the door with Emmet trailing behind him.

"We're not keeping him," Lucy reiterated.

"Methinks the lady doth protest too much," Wayne whispered and grinned down at the dog.

BY THE TIME WAYNE ARRIVED at the office of Evangeline Bon Temps, attorney at law, Emmet was sound asleep in the back seat of the truck. Wayne cracked the windows and walked inside.

Ms. Bon Temps secretary, Kimberly Reed, greeted him when he arrived. Kimberly was a soft-spoken young woman with ivory skin. Today her hair was gathered into a single long dark braid that hung down the middle of her back. She punched the intercom button on her phone and said, "Detective Nichols is here." The attorney was available, and Kimberly said, "You can go in now, Detective."

Ms. Bon Temps opened her door at Wayne's knock saying, "Please come in, Wayne."

Evangeline was a light-skinned black woman, slim with short dark hair. Although in her early fifties, her face was virtually unlined. She was casually dressed in black pants, low heeled pumps and a purple turtle-neck sweater. It was obvious she was not due in court that day. For court appearances she always dressed in a suit. Wayne had consulted Evangeline about a situation involving his foster mother a few years earlier and sincerely admired her consummate professionalism.

"I'm sorry to insist on an appointment today, Evangeline, but it's urgent. Sheriff Bradley asked me to meet with you regarding the estate of Mrs. Myra Cooper. His wife, Mae, is getting discharged from the hospital today and he's anxious to get her home and stay with her."

"As he should be. No babies yet?" Wayne shook his head and she went on. "I'm a bit surprised to see you, Wayne. The word is all around town that you and Dory both resigned from the sheriff's office." She tilted her head, looking at him curiously.

"I have, but I'm not leaving until the end of the year. After that, I'll be kept on as a consultant for major cases. Bottom line, Sheriff Bradley believes Mrs. Cooper was murdered. However, I've searched all around her house inside and out and there's no evidence of foul play. Mrs. Cooper was apparently taking her dog outside when she fell. The Medical Examiner believes that she tripped over his leash, and fell forward, dislodging her oxygen tank tube. Dr. Estes was doubtful that there was any evidence of homicide."

"I see," Evangeline nodded. "In that case, what can I do to assist you?"

"I'm aware that you're prohibited by your oath from revealing the contents of a will to any but the beneficiary, even in the case of a legal investigation."

"That's correct. I won't provide any information until all heirs are notified and I receive a formal copy of the death certificate. Then I can tell you about the will."

"Understood. However, I'm not looking for info about Mrs. Cooper's estate today. You handle real estate law in town, correct?"

"A good deal of it," she said.

"I'm interested in whatever information you can provide about the subdivision on Columbia Street. I understand the residents are being bought out by a builder named Scott Luttrell and his partner in the venture, a Mr. Pierce Turner."

Evangeline gave a slight grimace. "I'm crossing a line here, but I'll tell you in confidence, Wayne. I'm their attorney. Frankly, I wish I'd never taken them on as clients. It seemed straightforward in the beginning with the residents being offered a good price for their property and a right of refusal, but it isn't working out that way."

"Apparently Mrs. Cooper was on a lease-purchase for the house. Can you tell me about her rights under that sort of contract?"

"I haven't reviewed Mrs. Cooper's contract, but in the usual agreement, the title remains with the owner, or landlord until the tenant exercises his or her option to buy the property. In other words, this kind of an arrangement is a tenancy, not a house purchase. The agreement is identical to a regular lease between a landlord and a tenant, including terms such as the amount of rent to be paid, and repair and maintenance responsibilities of landlord and tenant."

"So, would you say Mrs. Cooper or her heirs had a legal basis to be able to remain in the house?" Wayne asked.

"Unfortunately, no. Mr. Turner who is the actual owner

of the property, would only have had to prepare a summons complaint and file it with the local District Court. It's illegal for an owner to evict a tenant without going to court. There would ultimately be a judgement and Mrs. Cooper would have to leave the premises. However, District Court is badly backed up at the moment. It would be six months at a minimum before such a case could be heard."

"Do you know how long Mrs. Cooper lived there?"

"Nearly thirty years," Evangeline took a shaky breath. "I need your word that you will keep this confidential," she paused looking at him intently.

"You have it," Wayne said.

"I know I can trust you. I'm pretty sure Mrs. Cooper was being pressured to get out."

"If she received such a notice and refused to vacate, what then?"

"Provided the owner had the support of the court, Mrs. Cooper would be considered a squatter and could be forcibly evicted." Evangeline gave him a sad look. "The sheriff's office would no doubt have to take care of that distressing matter."

"Interesting. Knowing this, I'm wondering whether Mr. Pierce Turner and his partner, Mr. Luttrell decided to take things into their own hands," Wayne was thinking out loud. "Dory believes that was the motive for the crime. With Mrs. Cooper dead, they wouldn't have to pay another dime for the property. It now looks to me like the Sheriff could be right that she was murdered." Wayne shook his head.

Evangeline's eyes widened. "I need to figure out a way to lose these clients," she said quietly. "One last thing, Wayne, you said Mrs. Cooper had a dog? What's happened to it?"

"Over my girlfriend's objections, he's currently with me. In fact, he's asleep in the back seat of my truck. We're trying to contact Mrs. Cooper's granddaughter to see if she'll take the dog. But honestly, I'd consider keeping him if it weren't going to cause a blow-up with Lucy."

Evangeline laughed. "As you know, I acquired a dog myself

after the murder in the Voodoo Village was solved.[3] I originally was reluctant to take her, but Erzuli has worked out to be a wonderful addition to my family."

"Would you be willing to tell Lucy that?" Wayne asked hopefully.

"I'm going to leave that negotiation in your competent hands, Detective," she smiled. "Good luck."

Wayne thanked her and left the office. He pulled out of the parking lot intending to return to the hotly-contested Columbia Street neighborhood and the house of the deceased Mrs. Myra Cooper. Even if he found nothing more that would help solve the case, he hadn't brought Emmet's food and water bowls home with him. He hoped seeing the bowls in their kitchen might further soften the defenses of Dr. Lucy Ingram.

---

3 Farrell, Lia, Five Voodoo Dogs, Camel Press, 2017

# TEN

~~~

MAE WAS DISCHARGED from Rosedale General on the Monday after Thanksgiving by her obstetrician who agreed to release her only after receiving her solemn promise that she would stay in bed for the next three weeks. Ben pulled his truck up in front of the hospital as the orderly brought Mae out in a wheel chair. The weather had cooled dramatically, and the wind was high, blowing crinkled brown leaves across the windshield.

"What are you thinking about, honey?" Ben asked, after ten minutes of silence.

"About three weeks in bed," Mae sighed. "Have you been taking care of the dogs while I was in the hospital?"

"I have, but when you told me the doctor said you had to go to bed until right before Christmas, I decided we needed to make other arrangements until the twins are born."

"What do you mean, other arrangements?" Mae frowned.

"I have boarded them with our vet for the duration. It's expensive, but better than worrying about you hopping in and out of bed letting them in and out and taking care of them."

"I suppose," Mae looked out the window, fighting a wave of sadness at the thought of a dog-less house.

"How are you going to keep yourself entertained for the rest of this time? Any ideas?"

Mae took a deep breath. "I had originally planned to decorate the nursery, but I guess that's out now. I'll just have to take it a day at a time. Lots of reading and TV in my future. I did text my mother and asked her to pick up some mysteries for me from the library."

"I was going to keep it a surprise, but seeing the expression on your face, it's time to spring it. I've asked your sister, July, to do the nursery for you."

Mae was overwhelmed with gratitude for her sister and her wonderful husband. "Thank you so much. With July in and out of the house selecting paint, baby furniture and fabrics, I'll be just fine. The only problem I can foresee is what color paint we'll use in the room. We don't know if these are pink babies or blue babies," Mae smiled.

"I'm sure July's thought of that and will have lots of good ideas," Ben reassured her. "It's good to see your smile. I've missed it," he took Mae's hand.

WALKING UP TO THE DOOR of her historic farmhouse, Mae braced herself for the silence, knowing there wouldn't be any four-footed friends to greet her. She was surprised to hear an instrumental version of the Christmas carol, "Joy to the World," playing softly. She and Ben walked in to see Mae's parents, Ben's parents, Matt sitting on Ben's mother's lap and July in their living room. A chorus of family saying, "Welcome Home!" brought Mae to tears.

"Take a look around, sweetie," her mother waved her hand at their surroundings. Mae had been so touched by her family being there to welcome her home that she hadn't even registered the fact that her house looked like Macy's department store decked out for Christmas. The tall artificial tree, adorned only in little white lights when she left for Thanksgiving dinner, was now decorated with every blown-glass ornament Mae possessed. It was grounded by a tree skirt with holly leaves and a Christmas train. The train encircled the base of the tree, occasionally hooting like 'The Little Engine that Could.' One of the wreaths she and her mother had purchased held pride of place above the fireplace and there was now a red runner on the mantle as well as tall candlesticks with white tapers burning. Little scenes of snow-covered villages and nativity displays were on every table and what looked to be thirty presents were under the tree.

"Oh my, it's just beautiful," Mae managed before noticing Ben's son, Matthew, coming toward her with a determined look on his small face.

"Matt has something he'd like to say to you," Ben's dad said, taking her arm and getting Mae seated in a chair. "Looked like you needed to sit down before you fell down," he chuckled.

"What is it?" Mae asked her stepson with an encouraging smile.

"Miss Mae, I mean Mom Two, I'm supposed to say sorry. I really am sorry. I didn't mean it when I said I wished you weren't pregnant.I promise to be a good big brother to the twins. My dad let me miss school this morning so I could tell you that." His blue eyes sparkled, and Mae laid her hands on his head, feeling his springy curls. It was the first time Matt had called her Mom Two and she was so touched she couldn't speak. At her silence, he said, "Now you're supposed to say you aren't mad at me."

Mae laughed. "Honey, I'm not. Really, I never was. It's just hard waiting for this all to be over and I know you'll be a wonderful big brother."

"I bet you wish you weren't so fat," Matt said.

There was a shocked silence, which Mae broke with a full-on belly laugh. "Matthew Bradley, you are SO right," she wheezed. "I'm just trying not to wet my pants right now."

On that note, the whole group roared with laughter.

An hour later, Mae was ensconced in her bed upstairs and everyone had departed except for July who had come up with her, and Matt who was downstairs talking to his dad. July was sitting on their bed holding her laptop.

"Are you up to talking about the nursery?" July asked. When Mae nodded, she opened the computer. "I've done a mock-up of what it will look like." She clicked on a file and a 3-D representation of the nursery appeared showing all four walls, two cribs, a dresser with a changing table top, two rocking chairs and mobiles hanging over the cribs. July clicked through the images, showing Mae a round rug in the middle of the room and drapes bordered with adorable hedgehogs. "What do you think?"

"July, you're just wonderful," Mae said and reached out to give her sister a one-armed hug. "Have you thought about colors at all? We don't know the gender of the twins yet."

"I've come up with two options. I've done lots of nurseries and many women these days want to be surprised, so I've run into this before. We could do a soft yellow with maybe a duckling motif on the drapes instead of hedgehogs. I saw that idea in the Booth Mansion Nursery. Or, we could use a pale sage green and have a feature wall with the outlines of trees. In either case, we would do the ceiling in a Robin's egg blue with white fluffy clouds," July said. "I've seen some small dog beds that look exactly like little couches that come in pink, blue, yellow and sage green. I think they would be cute to use for the dogs, so they had their own place in the nursery. Where are the dogs, by the way?"

"Ben took them to our vet until after the babies come. I'm sad about it, but it's probably for the best."

"You look tired, Mae," July said softly. "I'm going to go say goodbye to Matt and Ben and let him know about all the food that Mama and Joyce left in the freezer and refrigerator. Do you need anything before I leave?"

Mae stifled a yawn and shook her head. "Thanks Jules," she murmured. July kissed her forehead and slipped quietly out of the room. Mae let her heavy eyelids fall. She heard a burst of laughter from downstairs. Moments later, Ben's tall form appeared in the doorway.

"Everybody's gone," he whispered, setting her cellphone on

the bed beside her. "I turned your ringer off, but you can call me if you need anything. I'll be downstairs."

"What were y'all laughing about?"

Ben smiled and shook his head. "When I told Matt that his mom was here to take him to school, he told me he usually calls her Mom One now. Your sister and I were cracking up."

"Yep, he's a funny one." Mae winked at her husband and let her eyes fall shut once more. She heard him say goodnight and then she heard nothing more.

# ELEVEN

---

IN THE DAYS SINCE THANKSGIVING, the weather had turned cold and dreary. Rosedale's leafless trees had turned to shiny black silhouettes washed by continuous rain and occasional sleet. The entire village was decorated for the holiday season and Christmas carols floated repetitively from speakers placed around town. Several more houses on Columbia Street had been demolished, and the street was a muddy mess as Ben drove down it on his way to work on Tuesday morning. The yellow crime scene tape around Myra Cooper's yard flapped in the cold wind.

Over the last several days, Undersheriff Rob Fuller had been busy introducing the newly-hired Derek Harvey to the Superintendent of Schools and the Principals of the Middle and High Schools, as well as local doctors and pharmacists. Ben had assigned deputies Cam and George to patrol and jail duty, freeing Wayne and Dory to concentrate on finding anything that would support his single-minded contention that Mrs. Cooper had been murdered. Sophie Coffin, his office manager, was helping them when she had time.

Ben had waited until his sister-in-law appeared at the house before leaving for the office that morning. When he arrived at the office, he found his dispirited staff doggedly investigating the backgrounds of the two prime suspects, Pierce Turner and

Scott Luttrell, as well as Dante Jones who worked for Turner. So far, they were coming up empty. As the morning wore on, Ben's mood darkened and his responses to questions became curter and ever more minimal. After lunch, he asked Mrs. Coffin to call everyone in for a staff meeting.

AS THE STAFF FILED IN, Mrs. Coffin busied herself passing out coffee and Christmas cookies.

"Thanks for coming in, everyone," Ben said. "I'm going to start without Rob and Derek. They will be here shortly." He cleared his throat. "I know that, on top of your regular work, many of you have obligations to your families that tend to get more crucial this time of year. Plus, I've been a little grouchy." At this a groan emerged in unison from the group. "Okay, okay, so I've been a nightmare." He held his hands up. "Sorry. Anyway, I'd like to hear from all of you on Mrs. Cooper's case. You first, Dory."

Dory Clarkson, dressed in green leggings, an ugly Christmas sweater and an elf hat, rose to her feet. "I'd rather discuss my retirement party, Boss," she grinned. At Ben's weary head shake she sat back down with a sigh. "The problem is, we don't have anything beyond a motive for the crime. We lack a murder weapon, fingerprints, trace evidence, footprints or even anyone seen loitering in Mrs. Cooper's yard the morning she tumbled down the steps. I've been considering teaching Emmet to talk."

"That actually might get him Lucy's support," Wayne grinned. "The dog's still with us by the way and because Mrs. Cooper's granddaughter has gone dark, we're not getting rid of him anytime soon. I'm going to call her again today."

"I've checked alibis for Mr. Turner, Mr. Luttrell and Dante Jones. Turner and Luttrell were both in a meeting with the Mayor the morning of Mrs. Cooper's accident. They were in the room for two hours. It was a meeting intended to bring together the bigwigs in town to discuss opportunities for development," Dory's voice showed her frustration that their prime suspects had unbreakable alibis.

"Neither Luttrell nor Turner have police records, except for occasional speeding tickets," Deputy Cam Gomez added.

"We brought both those guys in for questioning—separately and together, and got nothing," Wayne said. "Even that idiot Dante has an unshakable alibi. He was meeting with Father Brice, the Episcopal priest. He really was, I double checked." He shook his head.

"How many of you think I'm chasing shadows here?" Ben asked, looking around the room. "I'd like a show of hands." Dory, Wayne and Deputy Cam raised their hands. "Well, I still think there's something. I get a funny feeling every time we talk to any of them. Like we're learning everything but the truth."

"I found something," George said quietly, and all eyes swung around and focused on their laidback deputy in complete surprise. "I've been covering the high school gym and cafeteria and yesterday after lunch I decided to check the school library for their yearbooks. Carol Anne Cooper graduated from Rosedale High School three years ago and Dante Jones was in her class."

"Now that is interesting," Ben said. "By chance George, did you check to see if they were in the same clubs or after school activities?"

"I did. Carol Anne Cooper was on the cheerleading squad and Dante Jones played football for the team. The yearbook from their senior year showed pictures of the senior prom with Dante and Carol Anne standing under a sign reading, Cutest Couple."

"Well, well, well, I believe George here might just have given us cause to bring Dante Jones back in for questioning," Ben said, feeling slightly cheered. The door to the conference room opened and Under Sheriff Rob Fuller and their newest addition to the staff, Derek Harvey, came into the room.

"We're discussing the Cooper case. Do either of you have something to contribute?"

"We've been pounding the pavements in Rosedale

introducing Derek here to everyone in town, Sheriff, but we haven't forgotten your certainty that a murder has occurred. We were talking about it last night and he came up with an idea. Go ahead, Derek."

"In reading Cam's report summarizing the neighborhood canvas, it struck me that Mrs. Cooper was out the night before she fell, playing Bingo at the Episcopal Church. The game starts at five-thirty and we only asked people whether anyone had been seen in her yard that morning, but not whether anyone saw someone in her yard the afternoon or evening before."

"Now that's what I'm talking about," Ben stood and clapped Derek on the back. "Between George and Derek here, we have a couple of promising new avenues to explore. Wayne, could you get Miss Carol Anne Cooper in the office?"

"Just one little problem, Boss. I've never actually laid eyes on Carol Anne and for the last week, she hasn't been returning my calls. Have any of you seen her?" Wayne asked.

Heads shook all around the table.

"We never suspected her of her grandmother's murder, so I guess none of us were focused on chasing her down," Dory said, shamefaced. "The one time I talked to her, she told me she was meeting with an Admissions Counselor at the community college the day of her grandmother's accident."

"I presume you double-checked that?" Ben asked. "People have been killed for less than an inherited house and Carol Anne was her heir." Dory shook her head looking embarrassed. "Mrs. Cooper was renting the house, so I didn't think about that."

"So, none of us have ever laid eyes on the girl? Did she even attend her grandmother's funeral?"

"I saw a young person, couldn't tell if it was male or female, wearing jeans and a dark hoodie standing at the edge of the group. Might've been her," Wayne shrugged.

"Do we even know what she looks like?" Ben asked.

"I took a photo on my cell phone of her senior year picture," George said and passed around his phone.

"Very good work, George. Okay people, here are the assignments. Our first priority is finding the missing-in-action Miss Carol Anne Cooper. Rob could you get on that?" He nodded. "Dory, I need you and Cam to go back to Columbia Street and talk to the neighbors again. This time we need to establish their whereabouts and anything odd they saw the night before Mrs. Cooper fell. Thank you for that insight, Derek. George, since you came through today in such a spectacular way, you get to track down Dante Jones and haul him in. Meeting's over, people, let's get to work."

Ben left the room with Wayne and the two walked toward his office. "What I need you to do is go back and talk to Evangeline again, today if possible. She told you she couldn't give us any more particulars until after Mrs. Cooper's funeral and all her heirs were notified. That's happened now. Thanks for attending the funeral with me by the way. You might see if Evangeline's actually laid eyes on Miss Carol Anne."

"You got it, Boss," Wayne walked away.

Ben went to his desk, sat down and pulled out his cellphone.

# TWELVE

---

M AE WAS SITTING up in bed, wondering if she had enough energy to get up, shower and wash her hair when the phone rang. It was Ben.

"Hi Babe. I have an idea I wanted to run past you. I checked with my son's 'Mom One' and she told me she'd never taken Matt to see Santa. A shocking lapse in parenting. I'd like to do something about that. Maybe this week-end. Santa's going to be at the bandstand in the park from ten a.m. on. What do you think?"

Mae didn't answer right away. Finally, she said, "Oh Ben, I want to go with you, and I can't. I'm missing out on so many things. Mom and July were going to give me a baby shower and now apparently they've even cancelled that."

"I thought you'd want to go with us and so I checked with your Nazi obstetrician. He said if I took you from the door to the car in a wheelchair, lifted you into the car, and you sat in a chair the entire time Matt stood in line to see Santa, you could go. I even checked the weather and it's supposed to be in the high fifties and sunny that day."

"That would be awesome. Despite July traipsing in with samples and deliveries of furniture for the nursery, this bedroom is starting to feel like a jail cell. A field trip, how glorious, I can't wait. You are just the best," Mae enthused.

"No, you are, but let's not argue," Mae could hear the smile in his voice.

With a lift in her spirits, thinking about being able to be outside in fresh air and sunshine, Mae was inspired to get out of bed. After a shower and putting on fresh pajamas, she made her way reluctantly back to bed. She could hear July's voice downstairs in the kitchen. It sounded like she was talking to Tammy, Mae's best friend since elementary school. The two came through the bedroom door moments later.

"Hi, you two," Mae said with a smile.

"I have a present for you," July handed her sister a beautifully wrapped box.

Untying the ribbon, Mae saw a pink quilted satin bed jacket. "Thank you so much, July. Where on earth did you find this? I didn't even know you could find these beautiful old things any more. It's vintage and so soft. What have you got there, Tammy?"

"It's my little travelling beauty kit. I'm going to do your hair and make-up," Tammy said.

"Goodness, you haven't done my hair and make-up since my wedding. I remember going to Birdy's Salon and you giving me the works before my first date with Ben. What's the occasion?"

Tammy gave July an oblique glance before saying, casually, "Oh nothing. Just thought it would give you a lift."

"It always does. Ben won't recognize me when he gets home, I've been really letting myself go since being confined to bed."

Tammy set to work and an hour later, Mae looked at herself in a hand mirror and was amazed. "Tammy, you're a genius. Thank you. Looking good always gives a woman confidence." At that moment, Mae heard her mother's voice downstairs talking to another woman that Mae thought might be Joyce, her mother-in-law.

"I have to get going, Mae," Tammy said. "Patrick has some big meeting with his major advisor about his dissertation, and only agreed to baby-sit for an hour. I actually object to the term baby-sit when Patrick refers to our children. After all, they are his sons," she said, rolled her eyes and breezed out the door. July said good-bye also, saying she would be back later to supervise the unpacking of furniture for the nursery that was being delivered that day.

Moments later, Mae's mother and mother-in-law both came into the bedroom. "Hello you two," Mae said. "What's up?"

"We come bearing presents," Suzanne said, and Mae noticed several bulging shopping bags. "I'm going to hand these to you one at a time." She proceeded to do so and in the next two hours, Mae's bed was inundated with gifts—shower gifts for the babies.

There were disposable diapers in every size between infancy and two years old that her mother had made into a "diaper cake" stacked in layers like a wedding cake. It was topped by two miniature baby bottles. There were onesies, baby teething rings, tiny bath toys, two bath towels and washcloths decorated with adorable little giraffes, a baby carrier for twins that was worn on the front of the parent's body, Thing One and Thing Two infant sized red-footed pajamas, and even a baby swing for twins. Mae was overwhelmed with gratitude.

"I finally get it! You're giving me a progressive baby shower, like a progressive dinner, where I get to lie here in state, and you come in one after the other and bring me presents. Thank you both so much. I feel like a pampered queen."

An hour later, after kissing her good-bye, Mae's mother and mother-in-law departed, chatting happily.

Later that day, Katie Hudson, Ben's former fiancé and biological mother to Ben's son stopped by.

"Hi Mae," she said keeping hold of her son's shirt collar to keep him from barreling into the room.

"Hi Katie, thanks for coming. I appreciate it so much," Mae said.

Katie had brought a picture frame for the first picture of

the twins. The inscription read: "Two miracles instead of one." Little Matt was trying determinedly to escape Katie's grip and climb up on the bed.

"He can come up here," Mae said, and Matt crawled up and settled down beside Mae who he had dubbed his 'Mom Two.'

"I have presents for the twins," he said proudly, and Mae unwrapped two miniature matchbox trucks that Matt had crumpled up in tinfoil. "They were mine, but now the twins can have them."

"You're going to be the best big brother in the world," Mae said.

"I know," Matt said and both moms laughed.

After Katie and Matt left, Patrick West, brother to Mae's former fiancé Noah who had died in a tragic car crash nearly five years earlier, made an appearance. He brought two black and white onesies that said "Little drinking buddies" above baby bottles outlined in white. Mae felt both euphoric and exhausted after Patrick left. She drifted off into a deep sleep.

BEN ARRIVED HOME AROUND SIX to find his wife with her long blonde curls spread out on the pillow. He had a glass of wine in each hand.

"Wake up, sleepy head," he said, and Mae struggled to a sitting position. "This room looks like a tornado hit it, a baby shower tornado."

"the Nursery is supposed to be done tomorrow, so I'll just try not to trip over anything tonight when I get up a dozen times to pee."

"I'll take all the gifts into the nursery now," Ben said.

"What's been happening at the office? Have you made any progress on Mrs. Cooper's case?" Mae asked.

"Had a break-through at the staff meeting this morning. The new guy, Derek, had a good idea. Apparently, Mrs. Cooper was out playing Bingo at church the night before she fell and none of us had thought to ask the neighbors if someone had been in her yard that night. Then George, of all people, figured out that Carol Ann Cooper had been Dante Jones' girlfriend in high school. Nobody from the office has set eyes on the girl. We're still trying to find her."

"None of the staff have seen her?" Mae frowned.

"I guess not. It makes me think that she's hiding out somewhere. Once we realized we didn't even know what Carol Anne looked like, except for a high school picture, Mrs. Coffin checked the phone log. She hasn't returned any of our calls since the day you got out of the hospital. As of today, she's been missing for almost two weeks."

"If Mrs. Cooper was murdered, aren't you worried that whoever killed her might try to kill Carol Anne? Especially if she's going to inherit that house," Mae said, her eyes opening wide.

"The house doesn't have any value for Carol Anne because it was a rental," Ben said.

"Are you sure about that, Ben?" Mae asked, frowning. "Dory told me the woman had lived there for thirty years."

"Pretty sure. Wayne talked to Evangeline about it. But that leaves me with the question of why Carol Anne would be hiding."

"Maybe she saw something she shouldn't have seen," Mae said, gravely. "Or she got warned off by somebody."

"Like Dante Jones for example. They were dating as seniors and could still be in touch," Ben said deep in thought. "Damn it, we've just got to find that girl. I'm worried about her."

"Doesn't she have a job?"

"She was working at a restaurant in Nashville. We checked that out today. She hasn't been in to work in a week. They had an address for her, but when Dory got to the place, she had moved out. It's possible that she did go see Evangeline, her grandmother's attorney, and if so, their office might have contact information. Wayne's going to go see Evangeline tomorrow."

"Doesn't the girl have a cell phone?" Mae asked.

"Yes, and we triangulated the cell towers that led us directly to a dumpster. When we called the number, we could hear it ringing. I made Deputy Cam climb down in there and get it. She wasn't pleased. It was an iPhone, but we don't have the password, so we couldn't access her call history."

"What about a car? Surely she has a car?" Mae asked.

"Yes, and we had an APB out on it. Rob found it today, abandoned in a Ride-Share lot by the freeway."

"I just had an idea. Since they were high school sweethearts, maybe Carol Anne is staying at Dante's house."

"Worth checking. But if Dante engineered Mrs. Cooper's fall, he could hurt Carol Anne too," Ben pointed out.

"Or maybe Dante's protecting her from your two prime suspects," Mae said. "Your chauvinism is showing, Sheriff. You admit to being worried about Carol Anne, but Dante's just a kid, too. He could also be in danger. It seems you were right to be suspicious, though. Something ugly is happening on Columbia Street and Mrs. Cooper got the brunt of it."

"Not just the brunt of it. Whatever is going on over there caused Mrs. Cooper' death," Ben said, and in that bright room filled with new baby things, Mae shivered. "Thank you for thinking this through with me, Mae. It's been helpful. I clearly married one smart cookie."

"Clearly," Mae grinned. "One very round cookie, to boot. Katie came over today and brought Matt with her. Those two beautifully re-wrapped tinfoil lumps are your son's presents for the babies. Go ahead, take a peek."

Ben unwrapped the tinfoil to reveal two little matchbook trucks. He chuckled and said, "These two were his favorites when I first found out I was his dad. It's actually quite a gift he's giving us. I missed out on so much when he was little. I'm not going to forgo those early years this time, Mae. I promise I'm going to be here for you and for them," he patted Mae's belly.

"I know you are," Mae said and gave her husband a kiss.

# THIRTEEN

⁓

EVANGELINE WAS SITTING at her desk re-reading the information from Myra Cooper's Rent-to-Own contract. She put the papers down for a moment and gazed out the window. It was overcast and raining lightly on this mid-December Wednesday. She was due in court later that day and realized she would need to wear a raincoat and take an umbrella. *This rain is going to ruin my new navy pumps.* They were tight on her feet and she kicked them off under her desk. Then she reached for the print-out from the bank showing Mrs. Cooper's payment history for the house. The substantial bottom line would be good news for Mrs. Cooper's granddaughter. She buzzed her secretary, Kimberly Reed.

"Yes?" she said.

"Can you try to reach Carol Anne Cooper again, please?"

"Certainly, Ms. Bon Temps."

"Can you also try to get Pierce Turner to come in to my office? I want to see him as soon as possible."

"Of course. I'll call right away. Detective Nichols is here hoping you have time to see him."

"Have him come in," Evangeline walked over to open her office door before remembering she was barefoot. "Good Morning, Detective," she said, feeling chagrined and hoping he wouldn't notice her feet. Spotting the grin on his face, she realized her hope was in vain.

"Come in and take a seat, Wayne. I assume you're here about the Cooper estate?" she said, quickly scooting back to sit behind the desk.

"I am," Wayne said. "Now that the funeral is over, the sheriff's office has several questions for you."

"Well, before you begin with your questions, I need to say that when I told you Mrs. Cooper hadn't accumulated any equity in her property, I was wrong. I hadn't reviewed the agreement or the payment history before we spoke. Mrs. Cooper signed the Rent-to-Own contract in 1988 and since then she made every rent payment on time. That in itself wouldn't change the fact that she was a renter, since she never obtained a mortgage. However, in addition to the rent, she paid $250 per month extra toward the value of the home which was at that time $85,000. And even more importantly, the bank has records showing Mrs. Cooper paid the property insurance and taxes on the property the entire time. Normally, Rent-to-Own contracts require the renter to purchase the home in one to three years, but that section of the contract was left blank. She had all the time in the world to complete her purchase and her payments clearly show an expectation of ownership."

"That changes things," Wayne said.

"It does indeed. In trying to determine the value of her investment, I used a house payment calculator on the internet. It isn't precise, of course, but at a minimum it seems Mrs. Cooper had paid off nearly the entire cost of the house before she died. I'm sure Turner and Luttrell would insist on litigation to prove it, but Mrs. Cooper definitely had substantial equity in the property on Columbia Street."

"I'm assuming her granddaughter, Carol Anne, is the beneficiary of her estate?"

"She is the sole beneficiary. Her father, Mrs. Cooper's son, died some years ago, hence Carol Anne receives the entire value of her life insurance policy, the whole of her grandmother's investment in the house, plus the contents and the dog—

provided she agrees to care for him."

"The dog, too? That will certainly please my frustrated girlfriend," Wayne gave a crooked grin. "Did you get Carol Anne to come in to your office? We recently checked and nobody in our office has ever laid eyes on the girl. Plus, she quit her job and moved out of her apartment. Even more ominous in my opinion is that we found her car abandoned in a Ride-Share parking lot. I'm beginning to wonder if Carol Anne knows something about her grandmother's death and has gone into hiding." Wayne took a deep breath.

"She did come to my office once, right after her grandmother died. At that time, I told her about the life insurance policy. I hadn't yet reviewed the contract for the Columbia Street property, so I didn't have that information to give her. I regret to say that since then, we haven't been able to reach her either," Evangeline's brow creased in a frown.

"Sheriff Bradley suggested she might be living with Dante Jones," Wayne said.

"Dante Jones?" Evangeline asked in surprise. "He's had some trouble with the law, hasn't he?"

"He has, but he and Carol Anne were a couple in high school. She could be hiding out with him."

"Hmmm. I know that Dante works for Pierce Turner and also does some work for Scott Luttrell," Evangeline said.

"What kind of work?" Wayne narrowed his eyes suspiciously.

"I got the sense that he collects bad debts for Mr. Turner. Those guys often turn to crime if somebody doesn't pay up. I'm sorry, Wayne, but I have another appointment."

"You might want to put some shoes on before then," Wayne smirked.

"You damn detectives are way too observant."

COUNSELOR BON TEMPS LEFT THE courtroom at four o'clock that afternoon. The rain had turned heavy and despite her umbrella and raincoat, Evangeline was drenched when she got back to her office. She took off her coat and hung it on hook in her entry. Pierce Turner was standing in her waiting area, looking at his watch. He was wearing a well-tailored gray suit, shirt and navy tie. To her surprise, he was holding a lovely bouquet of tropical flowers.

"I'm sorry to be late, Mr. Turner, I got held up in court."

"Not a problem," he said, smoothly handing her the bird-of-paradise bouquet. "These are for you. Mr. Luttrell and I appreciate all the work you are doing for us."

"Normally, I would never reject flowers from a gentleman, but this time I must." Evangeline's voice was cool and measured.

Pierce Turner raised his eyebrows.

"Come in to my office. We need to talk." As Evangeline walked past Kimberly Reed's desk, she tossed the flowers forcefully into the wastebasket. Once inside, she sat down behind her desk. "Please be seated. If you recall, I agreed to represent you and Mr. Luttrell in your development project on Columbia having been reassured of several key things. You gave me your word that you would not force anyone residing on Columbia to vacate."

"No one has been forced out," he said, although a trace of nervousness showed itself on his face and he tapped his fingers on the arm of the chair.

"Further, do you recall telling me you would compensate the residents fairly for their properties if they agreed voluntarily to move?" Evangeline's eyed bored into Turner's.

"I do and I've done that."

"There's some question about that I believe. Let me show you this bank statement. I requested it from First Federal yesterday. It shows that Mrs. Cooper paid off almost the entire value of the house at forty-five forty Columbia during the years she lived there. You may, of course, challenge this finding in court."

"As you know, Mrs. Cooper is now deceased, so I don't see the relevance of this information."

"I am well aware," she said, coldly. "However, her heir is

entitled to the value of Mrs. Cooper's estate. I personally have a suspicion that your urging her to vacate her home could have caused her death."

Pierce Turner looked like he had been hit with a baseball bat, but rallied quickly saying, "I presume the heir is some little upstart looking to cash in on this unlikely windfall. I'm fully prepared to litigate the matter. I assume I will see you in court, Counselor," he said.

"You'll indeed see me in court, Mr. Turner, but I will be representing Carol Ann Cooper. You are no longer my client and I am no longer your attorney, nor will I represent your partner Mr. Luttrell any longer. Please leave."

A startled Mr. Pierce Turner departed shortly thereafter, and Evangeline walked out of her office to speak to her secretary. Kimberly had pulled the flowers out of the wastebasket and was holding them.

"These are awfully nice flowers, Ms. Bon Temps," she said, wistfully.

"Not nice enough, Kimberly. I'm not taking them, and neither are you. I refuse to represent that miserable excuse for a man for one moment longer."

It was still raining outside, but standing there in the office, Evangeline could have sworn the sun was coming out.

# FOURTEEN

———

SUZANNE DECEMBER WAS SITTING at her kitchen island admiring the beautiful slab of granite that her daughter, July, had acquired when the kitchen was remodeled. She was having a cup of coffee and reading the paper. Her husband was making pancakes and humming tunelessly to himself.

"Listen to this, Don. It's the lead story in the Rosedale paper. Stop humming and come over here, will you?"

Don handed his wife a stack of steaming blueberry pancakes on a plate and sat at the counter beside her.

"It's an article by my colleague, Eldon Kohn. It reads, 'Sheriff Ben Bradley and his staff admitted today to feeling stumped by the worst robbery in a century to take place in Rosedale.' This is a quote from Ben, 'When Father Brice from All Saints' Episcopal Church initially informed me that the entire Christmas Nativity display was missing from the front lawn of the church, I thought it was a holiday prank. We have since learned that eight beautifully hand-carved life-sized human figures, worth approximately a quarter of a million dollars, have been stolen. Also missing are two young live donkeys kept in a pen adjacent to the Nativity display. The thief left a printed note in the manger. We are not releasing the contents of the note to the public until we thoroughly investigate. Evidence of sightings of any figures from the display should be brought in to the sheriff's office. As Sheriff of Rosedale, I pledge that the Nativity will be back at All Saints by Christmas Eve."

"Poor Ben. His butt is on the line now," Don shook his head. "If he doesn't get that Nativity back to the church before Christmas, he won't be able to attend a single Christmas Eve service in town."

"You sound doubtful," Suzanne was shocked. "I have faith in our son-in-law. I need to get busy writing my column for the paper. I was planning to do a story about the Christmas light parade, but this article changes everything. Stealing the Nativity. It's outrageous! Who would do such a callous thing at Christmas time? I'm going over to the sheriff's office now."

"Couldn't you just leave this one to Ben? I'm sure you remember what problems you caused by reporting on criminals last time," Don frowned at his wife.[4] "The poor guy's under so much pressure as it is with Mae threatening to give birth any day."

"You're digging your grave with that tongue of yours. It's Mae who is pregnant, Mae who is going to give birth, and Mae who is confined to bed. Men," she said looking at her husband in acute frustration. "You're all happy to say we're pregnant, but who is it that goes through pregnancy, labor and delivery, I'd like to know," Suzanne stood up. With her hands on her hips, even at five feet tall she was the very picture of outrage.

"Okay, okay. Sorry," he said. "Didn't mean to diminish Mae's part in this, but you women never seem to realize how tough this is on us guys."

"For heaven's sake," Suzanne said and turned to leave the kitchen. Her exit lost some of its punch however when the tie for her bathrobe caught on a cupboard handle, her robe fell open and she was left standing practically naked. "Don't say a single word," she warned her husband. "I assume you are taking care of Mae today."

Don raised his arms in surrender.

---

4  Farrell, Lia, Six Dogs 'Til Sunday, Camel Press, 2018

ARRIVING AT THE SHERIFF'S OFFICE half an hour later, Suzanne was stunned to see the parking lot chock-full of cars. Inside, the lobby was a scene of chaos. The phone was ringing constantly. Mrs. Coffin was dashing back and forth between grabbing the phone and trying to comfort Father Brice who was running his hands through his thinning hair looking terribly distraught. Deputy Cam was putting up a sign in the lobby saying, "Sightings of the Nativity Statues" with an arrow pointing down the hall. Deputy George was handing out pads and pencils for people to make notes on what they had seen.

Suzanne pulled out her press pass, walked down the hall and into the conference room. Ben, Undersheriff Rob, and Detective Nichols were sitting at the table taking statements. Dory was standing in the entrance to the room directing people to the next available officer. Suzanne touched Dory on her arm, crooked her finger and the two women walked down the hall to Ben's office.

"Whew. It's a mad house in here today," Dory said.

"It certainly is. Do you have any clues pointing to the perpetrator yet?" Suzanne asked.

"Well, the Nativity Thief did leave a note in the manger."

"That what I read in the paper, but Ben said he wasn't sharing the contents of the note yet. If you tell me what it said, I won't publish anything until I get approval from this office. I want to follow this story all the way until the statues are back on the church lawn."

"I probably shouldn't tell you, Suzanne," Dory lowered her voice to a whisper. "The note said, find the donkeys first. We're assuming if we can find the donkeys, we'll see another note. Ben doesn't think the statues were destroyed or that they're being held for a ransom payment. Rob seems to think it's sort of a treasure hunt. Whatever you find you have to tell me first," Dory warned.

"Of course," Suzanne smiled and hugged her friend. She had an idea already.

Mae answered the phone on the first ring. "Hi, Mama," she said.

"Hi honey. I'm sure you're following the story about the Nativity. It was in the paper this morning."

"I know. Ben got a call late Wednesday night and headed straight to the office. I can't believe someone would do this at Christmas. It's dreadful."

"Your father will be over there to see you soon, honey. He's bringing coffee and muffins. I just left the sheriff's office. Do you remember when you and Ben found that fawn lying in the field by your house last spring?"

"Yes, I certainly do. We named that adorable baby Pretzel because of the little white spots on his tan coat. That's when I learned about animal rehab. Until then I thought the word rehab only meant a place where people detoxed from drugs. Animal rehab is a service that feeds and cares for abandoned baby animals until they can be released into the wild. I also learned that if you find a fawn, you have to leave it in place for twelve hours before picking it up. That's the only way you can know it's been abandoned."

"When you took baby Pretzel out to Rehab, did you see what other kinds of animals the facility had?"

"I remember seeing lots of baby raccoons and a baby owl. Some kids found the little owl and took it into their basement where they were feeding it cheerios. Poor thing was practically dead when the children's mother found out about it. Owls are predators. They need meat! The children meant well, of course, but the poor baby was almost a goner."

"By chance, do they take donkeys there?"

"Funny you should say that, when I was there, they were planning on building a small barn meant to house farm animals rejected by their mothers, donkeys among them," Mae said.

"You can't tell anyone, but apparently the note from the Nativity thief said to find the donkeys first. There were two baby donkeys taken with the rest of the Nativity figures. Do you remember the address of the place? I'm going to run out there now."

"I have it in my Contacts on my phone. I'll text it to you," Mae said, and Suzanne heard her daughter whisper something quietly to herself about wishing she could go too, before they said good-bye.

# FIFTEEN

❧

WHILE ALMOST THE ENTIRE STAFF at the Sheriff's Office (and practically everyone in the village of Rosedale) was engaged in what was being called "Operation Nativity Recovery," Wayne Nichols had been thinking about Mrs. Cooper. With the revelation that no one in the office had seen her granddaughter, Carol Anne Cooper, and Evangeline Bon Temps discovery that Mrs. Cooper had substantial equity in her house on Columbia Street, Wayne was now solidly behind Sheriff Bradley's contention that foul play caused the woman's death. He contacted all his Confidential Informants saying he wanted a little chat with Dante Jones. Nobody had seen or spoken to the young man recently. After striking out with all his CI's, he got up from the desk, walked down the hall and knocked on Ben's office door.

"Come in," Ben said. When Wayne opened the door, Ben said, "I was just about to come down to your office. You said you were going to call your CI's to locate Dante. Any luck?"

"Nobody has seen the kid. I presume we're thinking along similar lines, Sheriff."

"Stake-out," both men said simultaneously.

"Exactly," Ben said. "I'd like to be in the car, but I promised Mae's mother I'd be home every night by six p.m. Who do you want with you?"

"Dory," Wayne said.

"Agreed. Given her supposed part-time status, although nobody could tell from the multiplicity of hours she puts in, I think I should ask her if she's willing to help. If she won't do it, who do you want?"

"George," Wayne said.

"Seriously, our Ace Deputy George?" Ben asked, looking doubtful.

"Well, he's the one who spotted the relationship between Carol Anne and Dante. Wouldn't mind giving him a chance to do a stake-out, as long as he's unarmed," Wayne said looking at Ben meaningfully.

"You got it. None of us want George brandishing a weapon around. I took his gun away from him two years ago. He hasn't passed a Qualifying Exam since," Ben said.

AS THE SUN SET THAT evening, Wayne parked his unmarked car across the street from Dante's address.

"Are we sure this is where he lives?" Dory asked.

"It's the info he gave us when we questioned him, but we need a confirmation sighting. I must say you have finally dressed appropriately for a stake-out," Wayne said, observing Dory's black jeans and black roll neck sweater. She wasn't even wearing earrings, a good idea since metal would catch the light. Then he spotted her shoes. "Oh, except for your footwear. Don't you have any boots, woman?"

"I certainly do have boots, Detective, but they're all knee-high leather, with stiletto heels. Thus, I wore ballet flats."

"Humph," Wayne growled. "Just hope you can run in those things. Dante Jones is pretty fast. I chased him once and he easily out-ran me."

Dory chuckled. "We're both getting up there in years, Wayne. If the kid enters the building, we best station ourselves by the front and back doors and trip him up when he comes out."

"Let's sit here a while longer and see which lights come on

when it gets dark," Wayne said.

"Did you know that Suzanne December, Mae's mother, found the donkeys taken from the Nativity set? They were at the Animal Rehab sanctuary," Dory said. "The little shepherd boy statue was there, too."

"I heard. When that woman gets the bit between her teeth, she just doesn't let up. I understand there was a note attached to one of the donkey's collars that said the facility had gotten a grant from All Saints' Church to build a small barn for farm animals but had never received the money."

"Apparently, there's a Religious Committee like a Board of Directors for All Saints' that gives out community grants. They'd been stalling on releasing the money and the place almost had to close. Suzanne was meeting with the Board today to get the money for the shelter released," Dory said. "Father Brice feels pretty embarrassed that it was the church's failure to provide the funding that led to the theft. Have we located any of the other statues from the Nativity yet?"

"Yes. We got a tip that something might be at the Senior Center. Rob's checking it out."

"Turns out Rob was right, it's kind of a treasure hunt, isn't it?" Dory smiled.

"And here comes Mr. Sunshine now," Wayne said, spotting Dante walking along the sidewalk. He was carrying a bag from the local grocery store and entering the old brick apartment building. A bit later some lights appeared on the first and third floors.

"Maybe there are mailboxes in the building with a listing of names. We might just get lucky," Dory said, and they exited the car. Inside the entryway they saw a row of mailboxes and the names of the inhabitants, except for one apartment that didn't list a name. It was on the first floor.

"I bet that's Dante's place. He probably hasn't lived here long or maybe he removed the name tag to make it easier to stay off the radar," Wayne said. He banged hard on the door and heard a male voice saying, "Hang on. I'm coming." The door opened to a big white man holding a can of beer.

"We're looking for Dante Jones who lives in this building. Do you know which apartment he's in?"

"Young black guy?" the man asked. At Wayne's nod, he said, "Third floor, I think. Are you guys cops?" Wayne nodded again.

"They always know," Dory said, gloomily.

"I just wish they didn't," Wayne said as they began climbing the stairs to the third floor. "Why do these old apartments never have elevators?"

They reached the third floor and spotted an older woman rolling a push-cart full of groceries down the hall. "We're looking for Dante Jones," Dory said.

"Apartment three-oh-two. Loud music," she said.

Wayne banged on the door twice before it opened revealing Dante who took one look at them, turned around and ran down the hall toward the back of the apartment. Wayne brought him to ground in the back bedroom before he could open the window and climb out.

"Okay, Dante. That's enough. All we want to do is talk to you," Dory said.

Wayne grabbed Dante by the arm, walked him back out to the living room and told him to sit down. "We're looking for Carol Anne Cooper," he said.

"No idea who you're talking 'bout," Dante said, belligerently.

"Now I find that interesting, don't you, Wayne?" Dory asked. "You can't remember your high school senior prom date? The girl in the yearbook standing with you under the banner that read, Cutest Couple?" Dory raised her eyebrows.

Dante sighed heavily. "What about her?"

"Tell us where she is," Wayne squeezed Dante's arm. "Don't bother lying to us. We know she quit her job, moved out of her place and left her car in a Ride Share lot, probably with the help of her high school boyfriend, right?"

"Right," Dante said, looking down and adding in a discouraged voice. "She's at my mama's house, twelve hundred

Gunter Street.

"Phone number?" Dory asked and as he read off the number, she punched it into her cell phone. When the call picked up, she said, "Mrs. Jones, my name is Dory Clarkson. I'm with the sheriff's office in Rosedale. My partner and I are with your boy, Dante, right now. He says his friend Carol Anne is staying with you. We'd like a word with her." Having heard that Carol Anne was indeed with Mrs. Jones, Dory told her to keep the girl from leaving until they got there. Wayne and Dory escorted Dante down to the car.

WHEN THEY KNOCKED ON THE door at 1200 Gunter Street, Mrs. Jones answered the door saying, "I wasn't about to let this skinny little white thing go, officer. Had to physically restrain her, but Dante's girl is right here. Come on in."

They walked into a house that despite its cracked linoleum tile and old furniture was immaculate. Carol Anne Cooper, wearing jeans and a dark green hooded sweatshirt, was sitting on the brown leather couch. Wayne thought she looked frightened and made eye contact with Dory, their signal that she should ask the questions.

"I take it you are Carol Anne Cooper? I'd like to see some ID please?" The girl found her purse and showed Dory her driver's license. "You've been ducking our efforts to find you for a while now, Miss Cooper. Both the sheriff's office and your attorney, Ms. Evangeline Bon Temps, need to talk to you. Want to tell me why you haven't been answering your calls?"

"Am I under arrest?" the girl asked in a quavering voice.

"No, but unless we get some answers pretty quick, we're prepared to take you in for questioning," Wayne said. "And we could decide to keep you in jail. Why have you been on the run?"

"Dante works for this guy Pierce Turner. Mr. Turner came to the restaurant where I worked and …he threatened me."

"Threatened you?" Dory repeated, frowning.

"He said I wasn't entitled to any of my grandmother's stuff

and I was to make myself scarce for a month or two. I told him my grandmother had left her house to me. He said he owned it, they were going to tear her house down and he didn't want any trouble. I got scared and asked Dante what to do. He said Mr. Turner meant business and brought me to his mom," her voice had strengthened during her brief narrative. Dante sat beside her on the couch, holding her hand.

"Ms. Bon Temps is going to need to talk to you as well," Wayne said. "I'm going to ask her to send someone to pick you up first thing tomorrow and bring you to her office. She has more information for you about your grandmother's estate."

Dory turned to Mrs. Jones. "We're going to bring Mr. Turner in to the office for some questioning soon. Are you willing to have Carol Anne stay here?"

"Okay with me," the woman said, and shrugged. "As long as she helps out."

"Thank you. I'll have an officer drive by your house several times a day, Mrs. Jones. Carol Anne, I need your promise that you'll say here until we contact you. Promise?" The girl nodded. "This is my card. The number on it is my personal cell and it will go right to me and nobody else. You are to call me if you have any concerns or if Mr. Turner shows up here. We'll be picking him up soon."

Carol Anne nodded, looking a bit less scared now. "Are you going to take Dante with you?" she asked.

"Yup," Wayne said. "We have more questions for Dante and what exactly he's been doing for Mr. Pierce Turner."

Both kids stood up and Wayne and Dory witnessed a teary good-bye before departing with Dante in tow.

# SIXTEEN

———

I T HAD COOLED OFF dramatically during the night and when Ben left the house, he noticed that each leaf on the shrubs by the back door was edged with crystalline frost. He shivered as he climbed into his truck. The scheduled interview with Pierce Turner was set for later in the day. He was a little apprehensive about it, knowing they had zero physical evidence to support an arrest.

Rob Fuller walked up to the door of the office from the parking lot at the same time as Ben.

"Good Morning, Sheriff. We scored four more figures from the Nativity Set yesterday," Rob said. He looked elated, his eyes shining.

"Now that's what I'm talking about," Ben said and clapped him on the shoulder. "Which ones were they?"

"First, we found the Three Wise Men. We got a call from one of the employees at the Senior Center. The note said that one of the gentlemen who spent a lot of time there had a heart attack and died. Apparently, his death could have been prevented by prompt medical attention. The city of Rosedale had agreed to fund a nurse-practitioner position for the Center, but the position was a casualty of the County's budget cuts."

"Just like our budget," Ben said in a discouraged tone of voice. "Good work, Rob. I'll call the Mayor today and see if he can find the money for the position before Christmas. You said four Nativity figures were found? What else did you discover?"

"Dr. Ingram's assistant, Channing, spotted the Joseph figure last night in the center of the garden behind Rosedale General Hospital. The hospital has been creating an outdoor meditation space for patients and their families. It's taken several years to design and build. The centerpiece of the garden was supposed to be a twenty-four-foot blue spruce that could be decorated for the holidays. Two years ago, the hospital put a deposit down on the tree from one of the Christmas tree farms outside Rosedale. Apparently, moving a big tree requires inserting several blades from one of those big mechanized tree diggers, leaving the blade in place for a few months, inserting several more, again waiting and only after about a year removing the tree."

"I'm guessing they never actually dug up the tree and the farmer is getting irritated," Ben said.

"It wasn't the tree farmer who was upset, it was the Hospice patients. The windows of their ward look directly down on that garden. All the terminally ill patients signed a letter to hospital administration some time ago expressing hope they would see the promised Christmas tree before their lives came to an end," Rob paused, clearly saddened. "The Rosedale General Board of Directors is in emergency session this morning with Dr. Lucy who is heading up the initiative to get the tree in place before Christmas."

Ben felt his spirits rise with the cheerful news. Only the Angel, Mary and baby Jesus left to find. Walking into the reception area, he asked Mrs. Coffin to assemble the senior staff and have them join him in the conference room.

"So, Dory, Wayne and Rob?" she asked.

"Derek too," Ben said. "The deputies need to stay on patrol."

"Right away," she said.

Ben paused long enough to give his office manager a smile, "Thanks Sophie."

Having grabbed his laptop from his office, Ben walked into

the conference room just as Deputies Cam and George were leaving. Both had wide grins on their faces. "What are you up to this morning?" Ben asked.

"Just a little surprise for the holidays, Sir," Cam said, gesturing to a small tree that had been decorated and placed in the corner. Three cling-wrapped plates of homemade Christmas cookies topped with red bows were on the table. Ben could smell fresh coffee brewing on the sideboard.

"Very nice, you two," Ben said. "Thank you. Did you hear that the Joseph figure was found last night?"

"Sure did. We're going to keep your Christmas promise, Boss," Cam said.

BEN SAT DOWN AT THE head of the table and opened his laptop. He clicked on the files for the Cooper case and his sunny mood evaporated. As his senior staff trooped in, everyone else seemed upbeat. "Okay, people, let's get started. Dory could you hand me a coffee? Pass around the cookies everyone. These are courtesy of Deputies Cam and George."

"George makes Christmas cookies?" Dory asked, looking at one dubiously. "Could explain the pudginess." She took a tentative bite. "Actually, they're really good. Try one everybody."

"For anyone who hasn't heard, the Joseph figure has been located and is joining the Three Wise Men, the donkeys and the shepherd boy at All Saints' today. Any other sightings or ideas we need to check out?" Ben asked. "We still need to locate the Angel, Mary and the baby Jesus."

"Since Mary is the patron saint for mothers and infants, I thought I'd go to the Angels Birthing Center and see if she turned up there," Dory said. "There's also a second article by Suzanne December in the local paper today calling for increased efforts to locate the remaining figures. The whole community is focused on the search. All Saints' is holding a special prayer vigil tomorrow night."

"Good." Ben said. "Anyone else?"

"Rob and I, with Lucy and her assistant Channing are going

to search the hospital tonight after hours," Wayne said. "The Joseph figure was found in the garden, but it's a big building. There could be more figures hidden there."

"Sounds like a double date to me," Dory said, raising her eyebrows archly. "Goodness, Undersheriff Robb, is that a blush I see?"

"Knock it off, Dory. It's not a date," Rob said, but that flush just wouldn't subside.

"Could have fooled me," Dory and grins spread around the table.

"I'll expect a report on the search tomorrow morning," Ben said.

"I'll want all the details," Dory said. Rob rolled his eyes.

"Okay, guys, I'd like to turn our attention now to the Cooper case. Wayne, I understand you and Dory conducted a successful stake-out, found the missing Miss Carol Anne Cooper with her boyfriend Dante and that you brought him in for questioning. What did you learn?" Ben asked.

"Dante was hired by Mr. Turner to get all the residents of Columbia Street to move out. As you know, the small bungalows on the street are being torn down to make room for mansions. If Turner owned the house and the inhabitants were renters, he stopped renewing leases when they expired. Then six months ago, Dante was given orders to evacuate anyone still living in their homes. If they would vacate in four weeks, he was authorized to provide first and last month's rent on a new place. That was usually enough to do it, but if they were still being difficult, he was permitted to give them a voucher for a local mover."

"Go on," Ben said.

"The process was working well until Dante found out that his girlfriend Carol Anne's grandmother was one of the so-called renters on the street. He talked to Mrs. Cooper and found out she was of the opinion she owned the property. She also said she had no intention of moving. When Dante told Mr. Turner this, he said he didn't want to have to go to court to get the house and to start putting the pressure on. He told Dante the old lady had a dodgy ticker, was on oxygen and probably wouldn't live very long. He thought a good scare would oust her. He went so far as to say Dante could threaten to shoot her dog," Wayne shook his head. "It was at that point that Dante grew a pair, saying he was dating Carol Anne and didn't feel right about it. Turner said he'd take care of it personally."

"Evangeline Bon Temps thinks Mrs. Cooper had a strong legal basis for maintaining that she owned the property," Ben remarked.

"She's prepared to go to court as Carol Anne's attorney and has dropped the Turner/Luttrell representation," Wayne added.

"We also discovered that Pierce Turner went to Carol Anne's place of employment and threatened her. Afterwards Dante took her to his mother's house. She's staying there for the time being," Dory said.

"What has come of the house-to-house canvas asking about the night before Mrs. Cooper took her fall?" Derek asked.

"I checked with our deputies. It turns out a neighbor, a Mr. Phillip Morse, saw Mr. Turner standing on Mrs. Cooper's porch at nine o'clock the night before her accident," Dory said. "It had gotten dark by then and he said Turner stayed quite a while."

Ben and Wayne smiled at each other, it was a "gotcha" kind of smile.

"Thank you everyone. Wayne and I are interviewing Mr. Turner later today."

MR. PIERCE TURNER APPEARED AT the Sheriff's Office before his appointment time. He was dressed in a very expensive suit and to Ben's dismay Rosedale's most prominent defense attorney (and Ben's opponent in the most recent race for sheriff) Ramsey Tremaine, was with him.

"Good afternoon, gentlemen," Ben said, trying to suppress his distaste for both of them. "Mrs. Coffin could you conduct

Mr. Turner and Mr. Tremaine to Interrogation?"

Mrs. Coffin gave her boss a quick look of surprise. Interviews with suspects were usually done informally in the conference room. Ben was moving this one to Interrogation right off the bat.

"This way please," she said, and the two men followed her down the hall. They were talking in low voices.

"Who's on point on this one?" Wayne asked Ben quietly.

"I'm going to start by threatening Turner with immediate arrest. You can chime in when Tremaine shows his true colors," Ben replied, turning up the thermostat that controlled the heat in the interrogation room. "Let's make him sweat." He grinned.

Both men entered the room. "Thank you for coming in today. We have a serious matter to discuss. We're prepared to charge Mr. Turner with the felony murder of Myra Cooper of forty-five forty Columbia Street."

Turner started to speak but attorney Ramsey Tremaine put a hand on his shoulder. "Mrs. Cooper died of heart failure complicated by the loss of oxygen. The cause of death is quite clear on the Death Certificate and I fail to understand how even a poor excuse for a sheriff such as yourself could have come up with such a trumped-up charge."

"Unfortunately for you and your client, Tremaine, we have three critical factors supporting our contention that the woman was murdered. First, we know that Mr. Turner, together with his business partner, Mr. Luttrell, are clearing the neighborhood of smaller homes in order to build expensive mansions and that Mrs. Cooper was refusing to vacate. Second, we know that since Mrs. Cooper had considerable equity in her home, evicting her would be both lengthy and the outcome uncertain in any District Court proceedings. Third, Dante Jones is willing to testify that Mr. Turner talked to him about Mrs. Cooper's medical condition saying that a good scare would cause her to move out of her house," Ben said.

"Furthermore, Mrs. Cooper's next-door neighbor spotted Mr. Turner on her porch after dark the evening before her fall.

He was there for quite some time," Wayne said, with a cat-who-ate-the canary grin.

"Hold on there, Sheriff," Pierce Turner said. "Yes, I went to visit Mrs. Cooper the night before her unfortunate demise. I had been there before and knew it took her a while to get to the front door. That's the reason I was gracious enough to wait for some time on her porch."

"That explains my client's presence at the home," Tremaine said. "With respect to Dante Jones, I can't believe the District Attorney will allow him to testify since he is a felon with previous convictions for menacing and assault."

"He's been questioned about several incidents. However, he had not been arrested and the charges were dropped. Believe me, he is a very convincing witness," Ben said. "And I personally believe that Mr. Turner giving Dante Jones permission to shoot Mrs. Cooper's well-loved dog would not go down well with a jury."

Mr. Tremaine glanced at briefly at his client. Turner shook his head. "Regardless of such hearsay testimony, the business of Mrs. Cooper potentially owning the home was not known to Mr. Turner at the time. Subsequently, in talking with Mrs. Cooper's attorney, we learned that it is litigable. This is now a matter for the courts. Let's cut to the chase here, Sheriff. You have no evidence, trace or forensics. You don't have a murder weapon. You have a post-mortem that shows the death of an elderly woman as being from natural causes. You have nothing but a circumstantial case. We're leaving."

"What we have so far is a persuasive motive with Mr. Turner moving everyone out of their houses on Columbia Street and Mrs. Cooper being the final hold-out. Furthermore, I just got off the phone with the bank and learned that Mr. Luttrell is heavily over-extended financially. Construction on half a dozen houses has begun, but only one is ready to go on the market," Ben said.

"Don't forget we have opportunity since Mr. Turner spent a half hour on the victim's porch the night before her death, no doubt engineering her fall," Wayne said with an evil grin. Mr. Turner was starting to sweat.

Tremaine looked irritated. "Regardless of the circumstantial evidence, Sheriff, you lack the means. You have no smoking gun and only the unsubstantiated testimony of a low-life criminal that Mr. Turner even wanted the woman frightened."

"Speaking of frightening people, Carol Anne Cooper, the victim's heir and granddaughter, is prepared to testify that Mr. Turner came to her place of employment and threatened her with violence if she did anything to stop the demolition of her grandmother's home," Wayne said. "She's meeting with her attorney today about litigating the home ownership question."

"Unsubstantiated testimony as well no doubt," Tremaine said. "Come on Pierce, we're leaving."

"I don't think so," Ben said, and his blue eyes turned icy. "Mr. Turner, you are under arrest for the murder of Mrs. Myra Cooper. You have the right to be silent. You have the right to an attorney, which you have exercised. Anything you say can and will be used against you in a court of law. Detective, please cuff our killer."

Ramsey Tremaine looked stunned but turned to his client saying, "I'll get you before a judge tomorrow morning and secure your release. Don't worry, Pierce. Don't say anything."

"I wouldn't count on a judge releasing you, Turner. The District Attorney is prepared to ask for remand," Ben said. Wayne cast him a quick doubtful look, but escorted Pierce Turner from the room after cuffing his wrists behind his back.

"You'll never make this stick, Bradley," Tremaine said, angrily. "Furthermore, I suggest you remove the yellow crime scene tape from around the Cooper house. Mr. Luttrell's real estate agents are having trouble getting people to tour the new home he has for sale on the street."

"In case you haven't noticed, Tremaine, it's nearly Christmas and judges and juries are especially reluctant to let murderers of seventy-four-year-old ladies and thugs who threaten the lives of young girls loose on the streets at this time of year.

My wife is due to deliver twins soon and I am in no mood to be trifled with," Ben Bradley said and added to Tremaine's departing back, "Hell will freeze over before I remove the crime scene tape on Columbia Street. There's something there and we're going to find it."

When Tremaine opened the door to the hall, a brief flurry of applause could be heard coming from the staff.

# SEVENTEEN

———

I T WAS FIVE O'CLOCK in the afternoon when Detective
Wayne Nichols and Deputy George Phelps pulled into
the driveway at forty-five forty Columbia Street. The wind
was rising, causing the yellow crime scene tape around Mrs.
Cooper's house to flap loudly in the air. Wayne opened the back
door of the car. Emmet lifted his head, sniffed in recognition of
his home, jumped from the car and ran up the sidewalk.

"Are the house keys still under the matt?" George asked.

"No. We thought they should be with us. Here they are,
George. I've got the warrant. I'm amazed the judge gave us one,
what with Ben jumping the gun and arresting Pierce Turner
without a heck of a lot of evidence. The frosting on the cake
was when the ADA agreed to ask the judge for remand at
Turner's bail hearing and got it."

"Mr. Turner's in the pokey until his trial now," George said
cheerily, as they stepped up on the porch. "The Sheriff said this
is our last day to find something."

"Yes. He's given in to pressure from the Mayor and agreed
to remove the crime scene tape tomorrow." Wayne looked
down with a frown. The dog had gone around to the side of
the porch and into the hydrangeas planted beside the steps.
The shrubs were moving vigorously.

"Let's search inside first," George said. Using the house key, he opened the front door that squeaked as they walked in. "What are we looking for anyway?"

"Something that would have made Mrs. Cooper take a tumble. Get your flashlight out, George and get down on your knees. I want you to look carefully at the area by the front door and on the porch. It's possible that Turner put something oily on the area. Look for footprints too. I'll take pictures of any that are not a woman's size seven."

"Why is it always me that has to get down on the floor?" George said gloomily.

"Because I outrank you," Wayne said, suppressing a grin.

"What will you be doing while I'm down here?"

"I'm going to check the medicines Mrs. Cooper was taking," Wayne said and walked down the hall to the bathroom. Opening the medicine cabinet, he pulled out five pill bottles. All had been prescribed by Mrs. Cooper's cardiologist. She had been taking ACE inhibitors, Beta Blockers, Digoxin and a diuretic. In the kitchen Wayne found over-the-counter vitamins, iron and calcium. She had no medicines on her bedside table, just an extra oxygen tank in the corner. Wayne dialed Lucy's pager number. She was at work and he hated to bother her, but she would know if any of the meds might have affected the woman's balance.

"Dr. Ingram, I presume," Wayne said when Lucy returned his page.

"Detective Nichols, I presume," she chuckled. "What's up?"

"I'm at Mrs. Cooper's place checking her meds. Can you tell me if all these sound legit?" Before she could protest and tell him to call the prescribing physician, he quickly read off the drug names.

"You know I can't tell you if these are appropriate for Mrs. Cooper's condition," Lucy told him severely. "I'm not her cardiologist."

"I just want to know if any of these could cause dizziness in an old woman on oxygen."

"Dizziness and nausea are common when a patient first

starts taking beta blockers. Is the bottle marked as a refill?"

Wayne squinted at the small lettering. "Yes, apparently a fourth refill."

"Then it's unlikely. Double check to be sure that she wasn't taking more than prescribed. I have to go, sorry."

Wayne pulled out his small notepad and carefully counted the number of pills in each bottle, comparing that number to the amount and date prescribed. Mrs. Cooper had taken her meds conscientiously. There was no evidence she had taken too many, or too few.

"Wayne, somebody's at the front door," George called out. "Shall I let her in?"

"Hang on." Wayne walked into the front entry and asked if George had seen any evidence of a greasy substance on the floor or footprints made by men's shoes. He hadn't. Wayne opened the door to a stocky woman with tightly permed salt-and-pepper hair.

"Can I help you?" he asked.

"I'm Effie Martin, the Neighborhood Watch Commander. Just checking on what's going on here. Since there's crime scene tape around this property, I had to be sure nobody was here that shouldn't be." The woman positively bristled with self-importance.

"I'm Detective Nichols and this is Deputy Phelps," Wayne said as he pulled out his identification. George showed her his ID as well. "We're doing a search of Mrs. Cooper's property."

"Do you have a warrant?" she asked, frowning. "I'm quite aware that you need one."

"We do," Wayne pulled it out for her inspection.

"I've heard that Pierce Turner is your prime suspect in Mrs. Cooper's death, and I wanted you to be sure to speak with our neighbor Phil Morse. He mentioned something to me about seeing Mr. Turner here the night before she died."

"We have spoken to him already, but thank you," Wayne said.

"Did he tell you that Mr. Turner didn't spend the whole

time on the porch?" she asked.

"He did. Apparently, Mr. Turner was on the porch around nine p.m. for a while and then Morse didn't see him for about fifteen minutes. Then he spotted him looking carefully at the porch steps before leaving," Wayne said.

"Obviously you've done your homework, Detective," Miss Martin said in approval. "May I come inside?" She peered around the door in avid curiosity.

"I'm sorry, Miss Martin, but since this is a crime scene, I need to ask you to leave the premises. I do commend you on your sense of civic duty," Wayne said, and the Neighborhood Watch Commander reluctantly turned to leave.

"Irritating dog, move," she said to the dog who was lying on the top porch step. The dog walked down the steps and again crawled under the hydrangeas. As Miss Neighborhood Snoop walked down the sidewalk, she pulled a piece of paper from her pocket and wrote down the license number of the unmarked patrol car.

"George, you were the one who talked to the neighbor, Phil Morse, weren't you?" Wayne asked, turning to his Deputy.

"Yup. He told me the same thing she said."

"It would have been dark by then. Did Mr. Morse mention whether Turner had a flashlight?"

"The porch light was on, so Turner didn't need a flashlight on the porch. Later when Mr. Morse saw him looking at the porch steps, he was using one of those little pinpoint laser lights."

Wayne gave George a severe look and sighed. "I don't think you put that in your report, did you?"

George looked guilty, saying, "Sorry, sir."

Wayne took a deep breath. "Honestly, George, this is a murder inquiry. Every little thing could prove to be important. You know we're on shaky grounds with Turner's arrest. The case is almost totally circumstantial. Now get yourself outside and crawl under the shrubbery on both sides of the porch steps. I want that flashlight. Or anything else you find."

"Yes, sir," George said.

"Hold on a second. Put on gloves so you don't get fingerprints on anything. I trust you at least have evidence envelopes?" Wayne asked. Looking at George's nonplussed expression, he reached in his pocket and handed him several. When they opened the front door to go outside, he noted that Emmet was once again lying across the top step.

Wayne frowned. "Come on, Emmet, go down," he said. But the dog refused to move, flopping his tail against the wooden stair. George stepped over the dog and went around the bottom step to check beneath the shrubbery. He checked the right and left sides before emerging with twigs and leaves clinging to his uniform.

"Sorry. I got nothing," he told the Detective.

Wayne raised his eyes to heaven. "Come back inside, George. You can get Emmet some food and water while I double-check." Wayne entered the shrubbery on the left. Shortly thereafter he backed out of the bushes and crawled beneath the shrubs on the right side of the porch. Then, he walked back up the steps, took out his cell phone and snapped a picture of the stringer boards supporting the top step. When he came back inside, he had a plastic evidence envelope in his hand.

"George, call the Sheriff, will you? Tell him we're once again indebted to Emmet and that I have the murder weapon."

Looking at Wayne who was holding an evidence envelope with two little screws inside, George frowned as he dialed.

"Mrs. Coffin, this is George. Can I speak to the Sheriff?" There was a pause. "Hello, Sheriff? Detective Nichols said to tell you he found the murder weapon at Mrs. Cooper's place. What is it? Well, it looks to me like some small screws. I don't get it, but we're on our way."

# EIGHTEEN

---

"LET ME SEE WHAT YOU FOUND, Wayne," Sheriff Ben Bradley said, holding out his hand. They were standing in the front entry of the Sheriff's office. Having heard the news that the case had been cracked, Deputy Cam, Dory and Mrs. Coffin had joined them.

Looking at the envelope carefully, Ben saw a length of clear plastic fishing line knotted around two screw heads. At first his forehead was furrowed and then it cleared, and he started to smile. Then he started to chuckle. "Now that's what I'm talking about," he said and pounded Wayne on the back. "How did the dog come into this? Tell me the whole story. Come on everyone, bring the dog too. Let's go into the conference room. George, since you already know the story, could you find Rob and Derek and ask them to join us?"

"Yes, sir," he said, but seeing the expression on George's face, Ben suspected he was still in the dark about how a murder had been committed with two screws and a three-foot piece of heavy gauge fishing line. "Oh, never mind, George. Come join us. I'll text them."

It was a windy evening and the cloud-covered sky left the room very dark until Dory flicked on the overhead lights. Derek and Rob could be heard coming through the front door of the office. They walked down the hall and joined the whole group. After everyone was assembled and sitting around the table, Cam passed around the plate of the Christmas cookies.

"You may begin, my friend," Ben said nodding at Wayne. "I can tell you can hardly wait to enlighten us."

"We arrived at Mrs. Cooper's house knowing the Mayor had ordered you to take down the yellow crime scene tape tomorrow and it was our last chance to find some physical evidence to nail our perp." Wayne paused. "Tell them what we did first, George."

"Wayne made me check the floor in the entryway to be sure there was nothing oily spilled there. I had to be on my hands and knees," he frowned. "While I was doing that, Detective Nichols went to inventory the medicines Mrs. Cooper had been taking. Then a woman named Effie Martin knocked on the door. She wanted to come in, but Wayne wouldn't let her."

"All right, all right, don't keep us in suspense any longer," Dory said. "Out with it."

"Miss Effie Martin reminded us that one of the neighbors, a Mr. Morse, had noticed our perpetrator, Pierce Turner, standing on the porch the night before Mrs. Cooper died. He reported seeing Turner looking at the porch steps. I would still have been in the dark about exactly how the murder was committed, except for Emmet. Here, Buddy, have a cookie," Wayne said holding the treat out for the dog.

"When Ms. Neighborhood Watch went to leave, she practically tripped over the dog because he was lying on the top step," George said, starting to look like he was catching on. "He was either there or in the shrubs on either side of the staircase the whole time."

"Yes, it was the pattern of Emmet's behavior that made me order George down on his knees once more," Wayne grinned. "Mr. Morse had seen a little high intensity light moving in the shrubs while Turner was there that night and so..." Wayne nodded at George.

"I crawled around in the bushes looking for the flashlight. We thought it might have fingerprints on it, and I was wearing plastic gloves so I wouldn't smudge the prints," George said smugly.

"It was after George emerged from the bushes, even though he hadn't found the flashlight, that I had the 'ah ha' moment," Wayne said.

"Because of the dog," George said

"We get it, George," Dory said. "Go on, Big Guy."

"What Turner had done was to fasten a length of fishing line to a screw at either side of the front steps, about ankle height. Emmet was trying to point us toward the fishing line and the screws. This loyal guy was still trying to help his mistress." Wayne leaned down to scratch behind the dog's ears.

"Poor Mrs. Cooper tripped over the fishing line," George finished up, looking triumphant.

"Leaving, I might add, a purple bruise-line across her ankles, which Dr. Estes thought was from Emmet's leash," Ben said.

"But which our smarty-pants Sheriff knew was evidence of a killer," Dory added.

"It would be nice to get a confession out of our perp and avoid a trial. Perhaps you would like to take that on, Detective?" Ben asked.

"It would be my pleasure, Sheriff," Wayne said, grinning. "However, it would be easier if we had DNA or even fingerprints. The case is still mostly circumstantial, and I don't want his attorney to destroy us in court."

"That's what our lab techs are for, right? Take the evidence down to them and see if they can help us," Ben said.

AFTER EVERYONE BUT WAYNE AND Dory had left for home, Ben asked for an update on Carol Anne Cooper.

"Ms. Bon Temps sent her Investigator over to pick Carol Anne up at Dante's mother's house today. They're starting preparation for the lawsuit against Mr. Turner which they hope will result in Carol Anne getting the value of the house, whether or not she chooses to sell it," Dory said.

"What's happening with Dante?" Ben asked. "I stopped by the jail to see him and Deputy Cam said he was released yesterday," he frowned, looking significantly at Wayne.

"Yes, well about that. I apologize Boss. I realize that as my senior officer, it was your call. When we questioned him, we didn't get enough to hold him any longer," Wayne said.

"Sounds to me like I'm not getting the whole story here," Ben said, looking at Wayne intently. "In fact, this sounds remarkably like some of the things my six-year-old says when I pin him down. Only a few days ago, I noticed my favorite coffee mug was missing. When I asked Matt about it, he said and I am quoting here, 'It broke'. I told him when he broke things he was supposed to say, 'I broke it, and I'm sorry.'"

"Rather than blaming it on gravity," Wayne grinned.

"Indeed," Ben said, laconically. "So, Dante, not being held down by either legalities or gravity, is now free as a bird. Why am I thinking there's more to this story? Would you know anything about this, Miss Dory?"

"Oh, I just might, Sheriff. You see, Miss Carol Anne Cooper has been visiting Dante in jail and begging for his release. On the day in question, Wayne happened to run into her and while trying to explain why Dante was still in custody, Carol Anne apparently burst into heart-rending sobs. Our resident cynic and hard-bitten Detective turns out to be a sucker for beautiful young women with tears in their eyes. Who knew," she grinned.

"Ah," Ben said. "Well, given what you found today, I'm inclined to forgiveness about the Dante matter. After all, I've been known to be susceptible to feminine tears myself."

"Since we now have clear evidence that Mr. Pierce Turner is guilty of causing her fall, Dante and Carol Anne are together again and most of the Nativity figures have been located, I wonder if we could set a date for Wayne's and my joint retirement party. Oh, almost forgot. Did I tell you I found the Nativity Angel at the birthing center? They have a bassinet in the front entry, and she had been placed there. So, about that party?" Dory asked arching her eyebrows and holding out the calendar.

"December twenty-third looks good," Ben said. "You, Miss Dory, may now go into full party-planning mode."

"I'll leave the party preparations in your hands," Wayne said. "As I said, Rob and I are meeting Lucy and Channing at the Hospital later tonight. We're on the hunt for the other Nativity figures."

# NINETEEN

———— ∼∼∼ ————

DETECTIVE WAYNE NICHOLS and Under Sheriff Rob met Channing Soldan in the lobby of Rosedale General at nine that evening. Rob was in uniform. Channing was wearing a red sweater and black slacks. She had a reputation for coloring her hair to match her outfits and tonight there was a streak of red nestled in her blonde curls. Visiting hours were over and the foot traffic was minimal. Lucy was talking with the security guard. She finished her conversation and walked over to join them.

"We thought you two might like to check Labor and Delivery as well as the Nursery and the NICU," Lucy said to Rob and Channing. "Security has approved you checking those wards while we check Pediatrics."

"Fine with me," Channing said, smiling up at Rob who nodded. "Let's go, Rob. OB is on the fourth floor."

"Be sure to open closets and look in storerooms as well as the sleeping quarters for the residents," Lucy said as the couple were leaving.

"Ask any staff you come across if they've noticed anything out of place or unusual," Wayne called after them. Turning to Lucy he said, "I got the blueprints for the hospital from the city today. Just wanted to be sure we checked everything."

"Is there some particular space you wanted to search?"

Lucy asked seeing the rolled blueprints in Wayne's hands.

"Only if we don't find anything in the Pediatric wards."

"Let's go then," Lucy said, and they headed to the elevator. "There are a lot of areas in Pediatrics we need to check including Ambulatory, Critical Care, Peds ER and the Specialty clinics."

"Sounds like it's going to be a long night. Where do you want to start?"

"Before we tackle Pediatrics, I'd like to go up to the Hospice floor. Do you mind?"

"Not at all. When my foster mother was dying, she had hospice care at home. It's a true blessing for the final days of a person's life. I didn't realize it was available in the hospital."

"Hospice care can be obtained anywhere for patients who have less than six months to live. It's focused on making the patient as comfortable as possible," Lucy said just as the elevator bell rang for the ninth floor. "I think I told you that a month ago, all the Hospice patients signed a letter to the CEO of the hospital asking if there was some way, they could install the big tree before Christmas. They knew it would be their last Christmas to ever see a holiday tree." She swallowed, looking moved.

When the elevator doors opened, they emerged into a dimly lighted lobby. Soft music played in the background. Clusters of tropical plants scented the air. A semi-circle of empty chairs stood near the floor-to-ceiling windows that looked down on the meditation garden. A light rain had started outside, making the rocks and paths in the garden glisten. Three men were installing tiny white lights on the lofty Christmas tree that had been planted earlier that day. One of the men flipped a switch and the entire tree was enveloped in a twinkling net of light.

"Oh, Wayne it's so beautiful," Lucy whispered. "I just couldn't bear to think that the Hospice patients wouldn't see it before they passed away." She had tears in her eyes.

"Congratulations, Lucy. You did it," Wayne said softly and touched her shoulder.

"I gave the Hospice patients my word I would do everything in my power to get the Christmas tree in the Meditation garden. Now we can check Pediatrics," she said, brushing tears from her face.

THEY RODE THE ELEVATOR DOWN to the second floor and began their search. Two hours later, having found nothing, Wayne and Lucy made their way back down to the lobby with its coffee shop. They bought two cups and sat down to wait for Rob and Channing. The space looked like a lobby for a new hotel, complete with art and sculpture. The gift shop was filled with Christmas gifts and flowers. Small clusters of artificial trees stood in the corners. The hospital had recently installed a grand piano, and a young pianist was playing a Christmas carol. When Rob and Channing walked in, Lucy asked, "Any luck, you two?"

"Not a thing, except that Rob asked me if I'd like to join him for a drink," Channing sounded pleased. "We're going to the little pub on Division Street. Would you two like to join us?"

"No thanks. We have to get home. Emmet is waiting," Wayne said. Lucy cast her boyfriend a long look.

"I didn't know you still had him, Wayne. I thought Carol Anne had picked him up," Rob said.

"Nope, still with us," Lucy added, continuing to pin Wayne down with her eyes.

"Carol Anne's just waiting until she knows whether she inherits her grandmother's house," Wayne said, defensively.

Channing put her coat on and grabbed her purse.

"Have a good evening, you two," Lucy said, bidding their fellow searchers good-bye. When they exited the lobby and were outside, she said, "I can tell Channing likes Rob."

"Girl's a sucker for a good-looking guy in a uniform, I'd say," Wayne chuckled.

"Just why is it that you rarely wear your uniform, Detective? I'm a bit of a sucker for a guy in uniform myself."

"You already know Detectives wear a suit and tie when on duty and casual clothes when they aren't working on a case. I only wear my uniform for funerals. You have just about replaced my entire comfy wardrobe," Wayne said, frowning, "I'm still searching for my green boat-neck t-shirt. I don't suppose you would confess to having seen it?"

"Honestly, Wayne, I can't believe you haven't let that go. Boat-neck shirts went out in the seventies," Lucy said. "Are you ready for home?"

"Just one more stop," he said and held out his hand for hers. They walked back over to the bank of elevators.

"Where are you taking me, Detective," Lucy asked, smiling.

"It's the one place in the hospital that hasn't been searched," Wayne said. When they reached the room he'd noted on the blueprints, it was behind a carved wooden door. He pulled on the handle. "Seems to be stuck." He tried again, unsuccessfully.

"Is it locked?" Lucy asked, sounding stunned. "I can't believe it. The chapel is always supposed to be open."

"Is this the hospital chapel?" Wayne asked. "I wouldn't want you to get in trouble for this, Lucy, so I'm going to ask you to go back to the lobby for a bit."

"Don't tell me you're going to break into a locked chapel. At Christmas?"

"Thought you said it was supposed to always be open. I'm merely making sure that hospital policy is adhered to," he gave her a crooked grin. "Are you leaving?"

"Heck no. I understand partners are supposed to have each other's backs," she grinned.

Wayne pulled a small leather case from his pocket. He inserted a metal pick into the lock and after a few scratching noises the door swung open. It was totally dark inside, but the scent of candles and incense was strong. Lucy went over to a bank of switches on the back wall and turned on the lights over the altar. It took a few moments for their eyes to adjust before they saw her. At the left of the altar there was a tall rounded arch. Inside the arch a flickering light illuminated a halo above the blue-clad figure of Mary, mother of Jesus. They stood there looking at her in silence for a few moments, caught by the figure's beauty and spiritual power.

"Way to go, Wayne," Lucy said softly. "I seem to remember a memo about a year ago stating that the Hospital was going to rely on local chaplains in the future. They let our hospital pastor go. My guess is that the chapel is locked unless a local pastor is in the hospital. I thought at the time it wasn't right."

"Clearly our Nativity Thief agreed," Wayne added. "Oh, here's the note." After reading it quietly, he said, "I think you're going to have to go back to the Board of Directors again, Lucy. Our thief wants the chapel open twenty-four-seven and wants it staffed."

"I figured he would," Lucy sighed. "It was only yesterday that I finished badgering the Board about the Christmas tree for the meditation garden. Now I'm going to completely fracture my relationship with hospital administration with more haranguing. Should we leave Mary here for now? Or take the mother of God with us?"

"How about we take Mary back to where she belongs?" Wayne said and Lucy nodded.

# TWENTY

———

WHEN JUDGE CORNELIA COCHRAN left her chambers at lunchtime, she was rubbing her temples to try and ease her headache. She had spent all morning presiding over a grand theft auto trial which didn't end until nearly one o'clock. The arguments had been interminable, despite her fervent orders to the attorneys to "move along". There had been no time to slip out to visit the local café or even nip down to the cafeteria. It was her least favorite food dispenser, but with no other options, she visited the courthouse vending machines. Her headaches were often helped by carbohydrates, but the sandwiches looked soggy. She chose an apple and a pathetic-looking cupcake.

Walking back down the hall, she decided she just had time to read her clerk's memo for the Cooper v. Turner Preliminary Hearing. Her hopes were in vain. Her clerk, Joe Rutherford, had obviously been lying in wait. He was a shiny new law graduate with a mop of dark curly hair. He had impressed her during his interview with his ambitious career plans, but on a day like this, she found his intensity fatiguing.

"Judge Cochran, I wonder if you had time to read my Memo for the upcoming preliminary hearing." Joe asked.

"I haven't had time, Joe," she said. "I'm sorry. As a matter of fact, I'm hoping to get through it in the next fifteen minutes."

"Since this is the first Preliminary Hearing Memo I've prepared for you, I'd like to know if you thought I did a good job. I explained what the case was about, the issues you need to address, relevant legal precedents and my recommendations."

"May I ask how long the memo is?"

Joe's face fell. "It's pretty long," he said apologetically.

"How long exactly?"

"Twenty-seven pages," Joe bit his lip.

"Right. Well how about you summarize it for me, keeping in mind that I only have a few minutes. Come along," she said, and her black robe swirled as she entered the office ahead of her clerk. She took a seat behind her desk and motioned for Joe to begin.

"The Cooper versus Turner case concerns a question of home ownership. Mrs. Myra Cooper, deceased, entered a Rent-to-Own agreement thirty-some years ago. Since that time, she made every rent payment, paid an additional premium each month as well as paid the taxes on the property. Mr. Turner wishes to re-assert his ownership of the property and have the bungalow demolished."

"Who is representing the parties?" Judge Cochran asked.

"Mr. Ramsay Tremaine is the attorney of record for Mr. Turner and Ms. Evangeline Bon Temps is representing the estate of the late Mrs. Cooper. Mrs. Cooper's granddaughter, who will inherit the property if you rule in her favor, will be present."

"Mr. Turner?"

"He is being held without bail in the Rosedale jail and has not petitioned to be present."

Judge Cochran sighed. "May I ask why?" Although the Judge was Sheriff Ben Bradley's aunt, she had just returned from an out-of-town trip and hadn't gotten caught up on recent events in town.

"He's under arrest for the murder of Mrs. Cooper, but I didn't think that was germane to the issue of who owns the house," Joe said. Seeing the expression on the Judge's face, he was starting to falter toward the end of his statement.

"Not germane?" the Judge asked in an ominously cold tone. "Not germane, Joe? In what universe would the murder of the potential owner of a property by the other potential owner not be germane?"

Joe winced.

"In your twenty-seven pages of recommendations on this case, did you address what would happen to the property at forty-five forty Columbia if Mr. Turner were convicted of murder?"

"No, Your Honor, but I think...."

"And in your twenty-seven-page memo, what did you recommend as the right course of action in the matter of who owns the property at present?"

"I first cited English common law on the matter which supports Mr. Turner," he said.

"You couldn't find anything more recent than the Twelfth Century?" Judge Cochran asked, in a disbelieving tone.

"I believe that contemporary Rent-to-Own agreements are unilateral and thus the landlord is contractually obligated to sell the house to the tenant, if the tenant exercises that option," Joe said. "However, I didn't see anything in the briefs attesting to Mrs. Cooper asserting that option."

"Did you not see her thirty years occupancy, giving the owner of the property an additional principal payment each month and paying the taxes as a de facto assertion of ownership?"

"I guess one could support that argument," Joe said, sheepishly.

"What is the legal standard which underpins the judge's decision in a preliminary hearing?"

"Probable cause," Joe said.

"What does probable cause mean in this case?"

"Probable cause means there is a sound basis for prosecution. Winning a preliminary hearing can be more difficult than winning at trial."

"Difficult doesn't mean impossible, however, and may result in the charges being dropped," Judge Cornelia said tartly.

"If that is what you have decided, is there a reason to hear the parties?"

"There is always a reason to hear the arguments, Joe. That's why it's called a Hearing. I never make up my mind in advance. Just wanted you to be able to effectively argue both sides of the matter. You can tell the Bailiff to call the case number."

As Joe left Chambers to inform the Bailiff, Judge Cochran took two aspirin, washing them down with cold coffee. She straightened her back, rubbed her forehead and entered the courtroom.

TWO HOURS LATER, HAVING HEARD both parties' positions, Judge Cochran cleared her throat and said, "Mr. Tremaine, as the attorney for Mr. Pierce Turner, you have made it clear that should the property be awarded to Mr. Turner, he plans to demolish the house to further the plans he and Mr. Luttrell have for the area, correct?"

"Yes, your honor," Mr. Tremaine said. "The new houses they're building will create an upscale neighborhood that will raise property values throughout the community."

Turning to the attorney for the Plaintiff, the Judge said, "Miss Bon Temps, have you asked your client what her plans are for her grandmother's house, should she be deemed the owner?"

"I apologize, Your Honor. No, I have not asked Ms. Cooper what her plans are," Evangeline said.

"Then I shall do so now. Miss Cooper?"

"Yes, Your Honor?" The girl responded.

"If I rule in your favor what are your plans?"

"I hope to be able to start a nursing program at the local Community College," Carol Anne said.

"The Judge wants to know if you're keeping your grandmother's house, not your personal plans," Evangeline said.

"Oh. Sorry, Judge... I plan to live there, even if I'm living in the smallest house on the street. I didn't visit my grandmother very much when I was a kid. I regret that now. My grandmother had a dog and that house is his home. I hope it will be mine as well."

Judge Cochran smiled at the girl. "The Hearing is hereby dismissed. The property at forty-five forty Columbia belongs to Carol Anne Cooper. Mr. Tremaine, please inform your client that Miss Cooper is not to be pressured to sell her property, not now, not ever." She banged her gavel on the bench.

# TWENTY-ONE

―――

I T WAS MID-MORNING and Mae and Ben were on their way to pick Matt up from his mother's condo. They were going to take him to see Santa Claus who was patiently listening to kids tell him what they wanted for Christmas at the Rosedale Park bandstand. It had been a bit of a struggle getting Mae down from their second-floor bedroom and into the car, but worth it. She was elated to be out of the house and looking at nature, even from a moving car window.

"What's the update on getting a confession out of Pierce Turner?" Mae asked her husband once they were underway.

"I delegated that responsibility to Wayne who was only too happy to take it on. We figured DNA or fingerprints would make him confess, so we gave the fishing line and the screws to our lab techs for analysis."

"Were they able to get anything?"

"Not a blessed thing, but Dory dummied up a lab report and gave it to Wayne to use in his interrogation."

"Is that strictly legal?" Mae asked, frowning.

"A bit of a gray area, but Wayne didn't show the report to Turner, just held it in his hand and said we weren't able to get DNA, but that Turner's fingerprints were on the screws. He still wouldn't give it up—his attorney Tremaine was with him and told him not to answer. So, after that we got a warrant Turner's car and found the screwdriver he used when he attached the fishing line to Mrs. Cooper's steps."

"Did that do it?"

"His attorney told him not to answer but Turner actually told Tremaine to shut up when Wayne confronted him with the screwdriver. He said he'd never meant for Mrs. Cooper to die, just wanted to scare her with a fall, figuring she would move into independent living after that. I think he thought that would get him off."

"So, you turned him over to the DA then?"

"We sure did. I wanted to get him for premeditated felony murder, but figure he'll plead to manslaughter. In any case, he'll be put away for a good long time. Signed, sealed and delivered, Mrs. Bradley," Ben grinned.

"Very nice, Sheriff. Changing the subject, what's happening with the Nativity search?"

"I'm sure you know that your mother recovered the baby donkeys and a note which hinted at the motivation of the Nativity Thief. She found the shepherd boy too, he was with the donkeys. When your mom talked with the staff at Animal Rehab, she learned that All Saints Church had awarded them a grant they desperately needed. It was awarded, but never funded. Apparently, two of the directors couldn't agree on the project. One of them was ethically opposed to Animal Rehab as a concept. He said that if a baby animal was rejected by its mother, it was probably defective and should be allowed to die. The other director said opposing Animal Rehab was positively Unchristian. Father Brice tried to mediate without success. After your mom found the donkeys, however, he met with the directors again. They have now agreed to give the Rehab facility the money."

"Any other figures shown up since then?" Mae asked.

"Yesterday we got a call that the Three Wise Men were in a closet at the Senior Center. They have now been returned to All Saints. Plus, Channing Soldan, Dr. Lucy's clinical assistant, was leaving the hospital the other night when she saw a man pushing a dolly with a large plastic-wrapped object on it. She spoke to the man who said it was a piece of medical equipment. It was only later she wondered if it could have been one of the Nativity figures. The next day she followed up and found the Joseph figure in the center of the meditation garden where the Christmas tree was to be placed. The tree was planted late yesterday."

"I remember Channing. She's such a cute girl. She came to the party at our house after your election. She had dyed her hair pink to go with her sweater. Detective Rob was still mooning over Deputy Cam at the time, but I thought Channing was attracted to him. If Channing is still single, she might be interested."

Ben made an irritated noise. He had said many times that Mae should leave the match-making to Tammy.

"Any others?"

"Yes, Dory found the Angel at Angel's Birthing Center and Wayne and Lucy found the Mary figure in the hospital chapel last night."

"That's wonderful, Ben, terrific work. So, we have all of them except one. I'm sure the baby Jesus will show up soon," Mae said, patting his arm.

"I hope so. We're only two days away from Christmas and I've promised to have the entire Nativity scene back on the lawn in front of All Saints then. I'm feeling the pressure," Ben said, as they pulled up in front of Katie's condo.

"Guess I have to wait for you in the truck," Mae said. She put the window down, grateful for the early winter breeze on her face. Sitting there quietly, it occurred to her that there might be a connection between the motivation of the Nativity Thief and the death of Mrs. Cooper. She felt she could almost put her finger on it, but then the insight disappeared, like a vestige of a dream.

TEN MINUTES LATER BEN REAPPEARED with his son. Matt was wearing jeans and a t-shirt, his back-pack hanging by one strap over his shoulder. The little guy was staying overnight, but because Ben was working that afternoon, Mae had arranged to have her sister July keep him until Katie picked him up. Ben opened the car door and Matt climbed up into his car seat.

"I can buckle myself in," Matt said, firmly pushing his father's hands away.

"Hi, Matt," Mae said, smiling at the little guy's strenuous efforts at independence.

"Hi, Mom Two," he said.

"Your dad and I have a surprise for you, honey. We're picking it up after you see Santa and tell him what you want for Christmas. Do you know what you want to ask for?"

"I want a remote-controlled drone, some walkie-talkies and a microscope. Dad said no to the drone, so I'm going to ask Santa for that."

Mae raised an eyebrow at Ben who winked.

"What are you going to ask Santa for, Mom Two?" he asked.

"I just want to have the twins for Christmas," Mae said and sighed.

"So, nobody will call you fat anymore?" Matt asked.

"You got it, Buddy," Ben said. He glanced a bit guiltily at his wife.

"Ben Bradley, you're supposed to tell him that I'm not fat!" Mae felt tears of vexation brim her eyes.

"Mom One told me that pregnant women are always emotional," Matt said, in a blasé tone. Ben reached behind the seat and gave his son a fist-bump.

"Ben, you're now officially in the doghouse and Matt, you're not old enough to give your father a fist bump!"

"Maybe I should be in the doghouse instead of Dad, Mom Two," Matt said, seriously. "I think I would fit better." After that remark, even Mae had to laugh.

They reached the bandstand area and parked the car. Ben went around to pop the trunk and get the wheelchair Dr. Lucy had loaned them from the hospital. Mae got out of the car slowly and carefully lowered herself into the chair. Ben started pushing her down the sidewalk.

"I feel ridiculous in this thing," Mae said. "People will think I'm disabled or something."

"Better than fat," Ben said, grinning.

"Maybe I could make a sign that says 'Pregnant' so people will know and not call you fat," Matt said with an identical grin.

"If I could get out of this chair, I'd smack both of you," Mae said, looking at them through narrowed eyes.

"Like Mom One said, emotional," Matt said

"You've got that right, son," Ben said and both of them laughed. Mae gave an exasperated sigh.

AFTER SEEING SANTA AND GETTING his picture taken, Matt and his father came back to the car.

"It's almost time for your surprise, Matt," Mae said as the car headed away from the town center. A few minutes later they pulled into the vet's office parking lot.

"Are we getting a new puppy?" Matt asked.

"No, we are getting your puppy," Mae said. Mae and Ben had gotten a basset puppy for Matt for his fifth birthday. "Cupcake has been staying here for a while and I know you've been missing her, so she gets to come home for the week-end."

"Cupcake has been living here?" Matt asked, looking upset. "In a cage?"

"All four of our dogs have been here because I have to stay in bed and can't get up to let them in and out," Mae said.

"Come on, let's get your pup," Ben said, and they entered the vet clinic. They returned a short time later with Cupcake. His little owner kept stopping to reach down and hug her. He looked deliriously happy. The pup had finally grown into her ears. They no longer dragged on the ground.

"Make sure to have her go potty before she gets in the car," Mae called out the car window.

There was a large open lot behind the vet's office and Ben said he would let Matt run around with the puppy for a while. "Going to try to tire them both out," he said cheerfully.

Mae looked on smiling as the little guy and his dog romped through the field. Even this close to Christmas, remnants of Goldenrod and black-eyed Susan's rose above the browning fallow land. She saw a pair of goldfinches feeding on the last thistles. Soon the weather would turn cold. Mae wondered if they would be lucky enough to get snow this year.

Once they returned to the car and Matt got settled in his car seat with his puppy lying sleepily beside him, he leaned down and whispered, "Cupcake, I've missed you so much."

Cupcake thumped her tail happily.

"I remember the day we got her," Mae said. "She was so chubby her tummy touched the ground. I asked you what you wanted to name her, and you said you were going to name her Cupcake, because that was your favorite food."

FIFTEEN MINUTES LATER WHEN MAE glanced into the backseat, she saw both Matt and his puppy sound asleep. She whispered to Ben that Matt was sleeping.

"Now that my son is dead to the world, we need to talk about names for the twins again, Mae."

"I know, honey. It's been a hard decision. I guess we've agreed if the twins are boys that we'll name them Wyatt and Cody. Are you hoping for more sons, Ben?"

"I am, sort of. Having Matt has made me more confident with boys anyway, but either would be good. I just want healthy kids and you back to feeling yourself."

"Me too. Matt wants them to be girls, though. He said he was his father's only son and he wants it to stay that way."

"It's a bit too late to change whatever we're having," Ben said.

"I found this list of girl Christmas names and wondered about Angel. Do you like that?"

Ben shook his head. "Naming a kid Angel would just about guarantee that she's going to be a little devil, I think."

"If they're girls I feel like I want to see them before choosing names. Okay with you?"

"Fine with me," Ben said as they pulled into the driveway.

# TWENTY-TWO

HAVING STAYED AN HOUR at Mae's house making sure her sister was feeling okay, July started gathering Matt's things together. She had agreed to take him for the afternoon since Ben was on duty. Little Matt had draped his blanket over the dining room table creating a fort. He was reading a Dr. Seuss book to his dog.

"Oh dear, I forgot about Cupcake," July said, spotting the dog. "I better take her with us today too."

"You don't have to, July. I'm sure I can manage to let her in and out of the house. I'm feeling up to it," Mae said.

"No way. You look pale to me and haven't moved off the couch since I got here. We'll manage. Matt, guess what? You get to bring Cupcake and you can both hang out with your cousins today."

"Thank you, Aunt July," Matt said solemnly. Mae and July smiled at each other. Everyone in the family enjoyed Matt's formal titles for them. Although July's kids called their grandmother "Zana," Matt always referred to her as "Mrs. Zana". He even called Ben's parents, "Officer" Grampa and "Nurse" Grandma.

"Your kids only had a half day at school today, right?" Mae asked her sister.

"Yes. They're officially out for Christmas break today."

"Rosedale Elementary, where Matt goes to school, got out last Friday," Mae said. "What's your plan for the rest of the day?"

"After I pick the kids up from school, I'm taking them home to change their clothes. We got a freeze last night, but the sun is coming out later and it's supposed to be in the fifties so I'm taking them on a hike along the Little Harpeth River on the trail that ends by the elementary school."

Mae frowned. "I'm not sure Cupcake is the hiking type, July. Bassets are pretty short-legged you know."

"Matt and Livi won't be walking that fast. She'll be fine. No worries." She handed Mae the television remote and a glass of water and kissed her sister good-bye.

Two hours later armed with a backpack filled with healthy snacks, the boys Nate and Parker, their sister Livi and little Matt Bradley got into the car. July set off the down the driveway.

"Aunt July, Aunt July. Stop!" Matt's voice kept getting louder.

"What is it Matt," she asked, stopping the car abruptly.

"You forgot Cupcake!" He sounded like he was on the verge of tears. "Mom Two said I was responsible for her."

"Right. Sorry, Matt. We'll go back." Back at the house, July decided to change into a warmer jacket and grabbed her blue fleece. After collecting the little basset and her leash, they drove off again. The sun had come out and it had turned into a beautiful day. Ten minutes later they arrived at the beginning of the trail that ended at the elementary school playground.

"Okay, kids. Nathan, you and Parker are going to hike the long trail. You both have your phones, right? We're all going to meet up at the school. It's three fifteen now and I expect the walk will take you close to an hour. If you beat us to the school, you can use the playground equipment or run around the track at the school. We'll have our snacks when everyone gets to the picnic tables by the school. Ready, boys?" Both kids nodded and at July's signal set off. She turned to the younger two.

"Livi, you and Matt are going to hike the short trail with Cupcake. I'm going to let you get a head start while I get my backpack, my phone and the snacks out of the car. Livi, let me check the charge on your phone. Okay, that looks good. Matt, Livi is in charge of you and you are the boss of Cupcake until I'll catch up with you. It'll just be a few minutes."

"Can we go down by the pond and watch the turtles when we get to the school?" Livi asked.

"I want to see the turtles," Matt said. "I love little turtles."

July had forgotten about the pond behind the school. A brief flutter of worry crossed her mind. "No. There's a picnic table near the pond. You can sit on it. No going closer to the water! Promise me, you two. The water is only about two feet deep, but I'm not sure Cupcake can swim. Pinky swear," July said and the two younger children obediently hooked pinky fingers with her.

"Come over here, Cupcake," Matt said and snapped a bright red leash on his dog.

"Let's go, Matt," Livi said, somewhat impatiently. She took her little cousin by the hand and leading the dog, they set off down the tree-arched trail. The sun slanted through the trees spotlighting the forest path. July watched the two little ones disappear around the curve and returned to the car.

Having grabbed her backpack, July decided to visit the park restroom before catching up with the kids. Exiting the facilities, she tripped over a cement curb at the edge of the parking lot.

"Ouch!" July cried out as she landed on the ground. She pulled up her pant leg on the right side and saw her lower leg was scraped and bleeding. She had a first-aid kit in the car but since the little kids were by now out of sight, she didn't want to take time to bandage her leg. She got to her feet and winced at the sharp pain that stabbed at her ankle. "Damn it," she muttered. It wasn't just a scraped leg. She had sprained her ankle. It had happened once before, and that experience taught her walking a mile-long trail with a sprained ankle would be torture. *I'll just call the boys and have all the kids come back here.*

She patted the pockets of her jacket reaching for her cellphone. Then her stomach contracted with a sinking feeling. The damned phone was in her other coat, the one she changed out of when they went back for Cupcake. She had no way to contact the kids. She pulled herself up holding on to the corner of the restroom building and took a deep breath before taking the first step. Every time she set her right foot down was agonizing. Grimacing in pain, July limped back to her car. *I'll drive to the school and meet the kids there.*

SITTING IN HER WARM CAR by the playground and taking deep breaths to combat the pain in her ankle, July found herself falling asleep. She opened her eyes with a start to a knock on the window, it was Nathan. He held a struggling Cupcake in his arms and had a worried look on his twelve-year-old face. July put her window down. "Where are Matt and Livi?" She asked.

"I don't know, Mom. Parker went to look for them. I thought I should put the dog in the car." He frowned. "Why are you sitting in here?"

She opened the door and said, "I sprained my ankle. Put Cupcake in the backseat honey, I'll lean on you while we look for them. We better go look by the pond." *My god, if something's happened to them, I'll never forgive myself...*

Hobbling along, she and Nathan yelled the kids' names but didn't hear an answer. Then she heard her daughter's voice. "Matt, Livi, where are you?" Silence this time. Then she heard a small giggle. "Are you hiding from me?"

She was so relieved she felt like she was going to faint. "I'm going to count to twenty and then I'm going to find you," she deliberately made her voice loud and teasing, not wanting them to know how frightened she had been. "One, two, three...."

She could hear both kids' voices. They were whispering but

the nearness of the water made the sound carry clearly. She heard Livi's voice say, "What is that, Matt?"

"It's a baby in some pond weeds," he said. July let go of Nathan and limped to the pond. Both kids looked up at her approach in surprise.

"You kids are both in trouble. Especially you, Livi Parker, you were told not to come down to the edge of the pond." She broke off her angry tirade when she noticed her nephew had turned his back to her. He appeared to be stuffing something into his backpack. "Matthew Bradley, turn around this instant."

Matt did but tucked his backpack behind him.

"Okay, let's see what you have in there, young man. Did you put a turtle in your backpack?"

Matt's eyes were wide and very guilty. He shook his head. July was about to grab the knapsack when Matt said, "Please, Aunt July. It's my father's Christmas present. I want it to be a surprise for him."

"I won't tell him, Matt. But you're going to hand over the backpack right now." When July opened it and looked inside, she frowned. She pulled out the muddy object wrapped in reeds, and looked at it carefully. When she stuffed it back in the backpack, she was grinning.

"Do you think he'll like it, Aunt July?" Matt asked, his blue eyes worried. "I want to give it to him on Christmas Eve."

"Honey, I think he'll be thrilled. In fact, I think everyone in Rosedale will be. Did either of you find a note?"

"I did, Mama," Livi said, handing her a small envelope.

July opened and read it carefully before spotting Parker emerging from the long trees. "Oh, good, we're all here. Have the walks made you kids hungry?" At a chorus of affirmatives, July told the other kids where Cupcake was and what had happened to her ankle. Livi went to the car for her mom's backpack and distributed the snacks. Afterwards, leaning on the shoulders of her twelve-year old twin sons, July made her painful way back to the car.

July called Mae around six. "Hi. It's me. I sprained my ankle again. I got it taped up at Redi-Care. I called Katie and she came over to get Matt. She took Cupcake too, she said she'll keep her until after you have the twins. Now for the big news, my daughter and your son found the baby Jesus by a pond behind the school. And even more news, I've discovered the identity of Nativity Thief. The instructions on the note said the person who found the note should call her."

"Her? The Nativity thief's a woman?" Mae asked, surprise in her voice.

"Yes, and I called. She plans to attend the Nativity Play at All Saints' on Christmas Eve. Once everyone gets seated, she has asked that Ben walk her into the church. Matt and Livi will already be up on the platform for the play. She'll join them. In case you're in the hospital by then, you need to tell Ben about the plan. The thief said she'll be wearing a purple coat and a red beanie. I sent her pictures of both the kids."

"The way this pregnancy's going, I might just waddle down the aisle beside them," Mae said, gloomily.

July laughed "Either way, it's going to be a day long-remembered in Rosedale."

# TWENTY-THREE

⁓

THE TEMPERATURE DROPPED sharply on the evening of December twenty-third—the date of the retirement party for Investigator Dory Clarkson and Chief Detective Wayne Nichols. Mae and Ben's unborn twins had attained an estimated weight of at least four pounds each and Mae's obstetrician had at long last agreed she could leave her bed and resume normal life. Plus, she could attend the party, provided someone took her to the event and brought her home. The doctor warned her, however, that labor and delivery were now imminent.

Mae was riffing on an old standard, both hands cradling her belly as she surveyed her closet. "Hey, babies, it's warm inside," she sang. She couldn't remember when she had been so happy. It was almost seven p.m. when her cell phone buzzed and she saw the handsome face of her husband, Ben Bradley, on the screen.

"Hi Honey."

"I'm so happy that I get to go to the party tonight. It starts at eight, right? Are you coming to get me soon?" She was so excited to be out of bed that her words ran together, without any pauses for Ben's answers.

"Sweetheart, there's been a change in plans."

Mae felt her spirits crash. Normally a "change in plans"

meant Ben was busy chasing some criminal and wouldn't be home for hours. She took a calming breath and waited.

"Did you hear me, Hon? I should be there within an hour. I have to get Dory a going-away present. Apparently, I should have thought of this a while ago. Do you have any ideas?"

Mae swallowed, telling herself that Ben was still coming, just a little later than she had hoped. "Dory loves shoe shopping at Mercy Me Shoes in Rosedale. I'll call them. I'm sure the sales staff will know what she wants and her shoe size. What about Wayne, did you get him something?"

"I ordered a watch for him from Quentin's Estate Jewelry. Had it engraved with the dates of his employment with the Sheriff's Office."

"Sounds good. Come soon, will you?" Mae said wistfully.

"As soon as I can, Sweetheart," he answered.

After hanging up, Mae called the shoe store and asked them what Dory Clarkson had on her Christmas Wish list. They said she had been positively mooning over a pair of red Ferragamo stilettos. Mae had them held for Ben, cringing a bit at the price. Miss Dory had expensive tastes.

BY THE TIME MAE FOUND a black maternity dress that didn't make her look enormous, added a long gold necklace and her ruby earrings, dug some black flats from under the pile of shoes in the closet and put her hair into an up-do, she was ready to party. She walked downstairs carefully, holding on to the railing and went into the kitchen. Looking out the kitchen window she was astounded to see that it was actually snowing. Tennessee snowstorms usually didn't amount to much. The flakes were drifting down so slowly, they seemed suspended in the air. Mae smiled, finding the snowflakes sweetly disarming. Then she heard the wind pick up and the snow swirled wildly around the house.

Walking out to the living room, Mae took a look out the front window. The wind was howling so loud by now, she could hear it inside the house. The bellies of the clouds were blue-black and the slender poplar trees across the road were blown nearly horizontal. She clicked the television on, wanting to check the weather forecast. The announcer was saying they could expect three inches of snow before morning. The high winds were the remnants of a hurricane that had hit the Gulf Coast several days earlier.

A sudden cracking sound made Mae turn toward the window in time to see the big maple tree in their front yard fall over, almost in slow motion. As it fell, the tree hit their power lines, taking them down in a bright crackle of electricity. All the sounds of electric appliances in the house faded away. Instantly, Mae was in total darkness. She felt goosebumps on her arms. Her breathing came in short ragged bursts. Trying to control her fears, she walked unsteadily to the kitchen table and sat down. As she did so, she heard a soft sound like something falling onto the rug under the table.

Her back was aching, and she remembered the instructor from the pre-natal class saying some women's labor pains started in their backs. She felt her stomach. The twins weren't moving, another sign of incipient labor. *But my water hasn't broken, and my due date is still ten days away,* she told herself. But she couldn't help envisioning giving birth alone in a darkened house. It was a terrifying prospect. Her breathing quickened and her heart beat fast. She sat at the kitchen table for what seemed like an hour, sipping a cold cup of coffee. She felt a sudden sharp stab of pain in her lower back.

It was crazy to take risks at this point. She wouldn't wait any longer. She'd call 911. But reaching into her pocket in the dark she couldn't feel her phone. It had been in the shallow pocket of her black dress. The sound she heard earlier must have been her phone falling to the floor and as ungainly as she was, she'd never find it in the dark. She started to cry. She continued crying for some time before telling herself firmly, "Don't you dare panic. Just sit still and wait. Ben's coming. He won't fail you. He promised."

"Mae, are you here? Are you okay?" Ben called out frantically from the back door.

"I'm on the couch," she replied from the darkness. "The power is out."

"I could tell when I turned on to our road. The whole neighborhood's dark. God, I'm so sorry I'm late. I sent you a text, but I wasn't sure you got it."

"My phone fell out of my pocket on to the floor, it's somewhere on the floor and I couldn't reach it. I've never been so scared in all my life. I was terrified I was going into labor. I'm still shaking." She reached for Ben's hand. "No phone, nobody I could call. If I'd found my phone, I was going to call 911. Where were you for so long?" Ben reached for her, feeling her shake with fear and frustration.

He held her hand and led her to the couch. He had a hard time catching his breath, feeling his own fears match hers. He wrapped his arms around her. It had been a narrow escape, and all for two presents. He could have kicked himself. "Mae, do you want me to take you to the hospital now?"

"No. The pain stopped. And my water hasn't broken. I'm still upset though."

"Upset with me? Because I was late?"

"Yes, I just felt so scared thinking you were out shopping when I needed you here!" Ben could feel her trembling. He wondered if she was going into shock and grabbed for the blanket on the back of the couch and wrapped it around her.

"I feel just terrible. I'm not leaving you again until the babies are born. I give you my word, please forgive me. Can you?" He sat in the dark for a long time, waiting for her reply.

She took a deep breath before saying, "Well, since you're here now and I didn't go into labor, I guess I forgive you, but I swear if I'd gone into labor alone in the dark, Ben Bradley, I might never have gotten over it."

Ben gave a sigh of relief. "I wouldn't blame you. Not one little bit. Thank you, Love. Do you still want to go to the party?"

Mae's breathing was shaky, but she said, "Give me a minute

and a glass of water, will you? And find my phone. Then I'll need a hand up, and we can go to the party."

THE RETIREMENT PARTY FOR DORY and Wayne was being held at the Rosedale Hotel. One end of the room was set with round tables topped with green tablecloths and red poinsettia plants. Undersheriff Rob was pouring drinks at the Open Bar on the right side. Channing Soldan, wearing a dressy black pantsuit with a silver streak in her hair was assisting him. They were both smiling. The other end of the room had rows of chairs facing a large projection screen. There was a continuous slide show with pictures of both Wayne and Dory. Dory had included several pictures of herself trying on clothes as a toddler. Even at the age of three, she was a little fashionista. Mae saw one picture of Ben as a little boy holding his father's hand, standing by a young Dory's desk.

When Mae and Ben walked in the room exploded with cheers and clapping.

"We wondered if you two were ever going to arrive," Dory said and hugged her boss. She was wearing a floor length red velvet gown with a plunging neckline. Her boyfriend, Al, a good-looking black man, was wearing a tux. "Look who's here, everyone."

Mae greeted the members of the staff, hugged Wayne and Lucy, and looked around the room. Practically everyone in Rosedale seemed to be in attendance. Deputy Cam was there with her girlfriend, Captain Paula, from the Nashville Police Post. Tammy and Patrick were standing by the bar drinking champagne. Tammy looked as glamorous as ever, although her silky blue dress was a smidge tight. Patrick looked like an exhausted new father was supposed to, with dark circles under his eyes. Ben's and Mae's parents were chatting in a corner with her sister, July, who was sitting with her bandaged ankle up on a stool. Attorney Evangeline Bon Temps and her handsome husband, Jason, were chatting with Ben's office manager Sophie Coffin. All their friends had come out to celebrate Wayne and

Dory's retirement and wish them well as they entered the next stage of their lives. Judge Cornelia Cochran, Ben's aunt, was chatting with a young girl. The two of them walked over and the Judge introduced Carol Anne Cooper to Mae.

"Thanks to the Judge, I'm inheriting my grandmother's house. I can have her dog, Emmett, live with me," Carol Anne said, smiling.

"I'm so happy for you, Carol Anne," Mae said, taking the girl's hand and hugging Ben's aunt.

"Could I have your attention, everyone?" Ben asked from the front of the room. "First I'd like to thank my whole staff who somewhat reluctantly believed me when I said Mrs. Cooper had been the victim of foul play. We now have the culprit in jail where he is going to be for a long, long time," he smiled at Carol Anne Cooper.

"Second, the whole town really came together to help locate the Nativity display for All Saints'. All the figures, except the baby Jesus, have now been returned. We still have Christmas Eve to go and my wife hinted on the drive over here that she has faith Jesus will be at the church tomorrow afternoon. Apparently my six-year-old son Matt and his cousin Livi are somehow involved. My wife's sister, July, has already identified the Nativity Thief." Looks of amazement and sounds of clapping ran around the room. July took a bow from her sitting position.

"The Thief will be speaking to the town at the Christmas Eve service tomorrow," Ben continued. "Now, since even my very pregnant wife has an alcoholic beverage in her hands, I'd like to propose two toasts. The first one is to Wayne, my partner in crime, my best friend and the best man at my wedding. Please raise your glasses everyone. To Chief Detective Wayne Nichols." Ben looked directly at Wayne and said, "My heart is as full as my glass tonight." He cleared his throat and said,

"May you have the hindsight to know where you've been, the foresight to know where you are going, and the insight to know when you've gone too far."

Everyone cheered and Mae kissed Wayne on his somewhat prickly cheek.

"Now for Dory," Ben continued. "As everyone here knows, Dory is going to remain on a part-time basis to boss me around, attend staff meetings, and be a consultant to the Sheriff's Office. I struggled with this toast because this woman is so important to me. I hope I got it right. Here goes. Please raise your glasses, people. Dory Clarkson, you've given me some gray hairs along the way and it really annoys me that you don't seem to have any." Ben narrowed his eyes at her before saying, "To goodbyes—may they never be spoken. To friendships— may they never be broken. To Miss Dory Clarkson, everyone," Ben said and hugged her hard. To Mae's surprise, the resolute Dory Clarkson burst into tears of happiness.

SEVERAL HOURS LATER, MAE AND Ben bid good-bye to the last of the attendees and walked out to the car. The blizzard had passed through and they could see the stars. It was cold and soft snowflakes were falling intermittently. All the light posts in Rosedale had been wrapped in strings of white lights. The large tree in the square was alight. The town looked like a peaceful Christmas card. They could see the gazebo where Matt had asked Santa for a drone just a few days before.

"Our little town is so beautiful this time of year," Mae beamed. A few minutes later she added, "July gave me the Nativity Thief's number. I called and talked to her. I need you to reassure me that she won't be prosecuted for her crimes. There was a good reason she took the display, and everything's been returned." She looked at Ben intently.

"I had the same thought. I spoke to Father Brice, and he's not pressing charges. In fact, he said he met with the Nativity thief in person and they've planned a joint presentation for tomorrow, after the little kids perform the Nativity play."

"That's great." She leaned on Ben's shoulder. "Take me home, please, Sheriff."

# TWENTY-FOUR

---

CHRISTMAS EVE DAWNED bright and sunny, with sparkling snow blanketing the yard from the previous night's storm. It was a beautiful morning, but unfortunately the power was still out. Ben had dragged their mattress downstairs to the living room the night before, and they'd slept in front of the fireplace. The soft flames kept them warm and the scent of apple wood recalled summer bonfires. Ben, dressed in his boxers, was trying to heat up some left-over coffee on the gas stove. He was grumbling that he needed kitchen matches to light the burner on the range and couldn't find them.

"Kitchen junk drawer," Mae reminded him before calling Katie's cell.

"Hello," Katie's voice sounded sleepy.

"Hi. Sorry if I woke you. Just wanted to be sure you were bringing Matt in his shepherd's boy costume to All Saints' today by four. He needs to be there an hour before the service. You're taking him home with you afterwards, right?"

"We are. He's wearing a tunic, shorts and holding a shepherd's crook. Luckily his sandals from last summer still fit. He says he has to bring his backpack. Something about Ben's Christmas gift."

"I understand he plans to present it to his father at the Church. If you can stand not peeking, I think it will be a nice surprise."

"Okay, and Mae, I'll say a prayer for you today that the birth goes well," Katie said in her soft voice and ended the call. *I'm so glad we've become friends.*

Ben came back into the living room with two mugs that smelled strongly of burnt coffee. "I almost went into town this morning to get us some breakfast, but I'm never leaving you alone again. We might starve, but I'm keeping my promise." Ben's determined face made Mae smile.

The couple were still sitting on the mattress sipping the bitter dregs when they heard a knock on the door. Ben grabbed his pants and called, "Hang on a minute." When he opened the door, it was Wayne and Lucy. Their house was out of power as well, but they had driven into town and returned with coffee, fruit and muffins to share.

"What fun, a picnic after a sleep-over," Lucy said, walking into the living room as she shed her coat and boots. "How are you feeling, Mae?"

"Like I'm never, ever going to have these babies! I have a favor to ask, Lucy. Last night all I could do was strip off my clothes. Could you go upstairs to my closet and get my clothes for today? I left the outfit on the chair in the bedroom."

"Of course, no problem," Lucy said. "From what Ben said last night, I gather the Nativity Thief is going to be unmasked tonight at All Saints'. Can you give me a hint about what's going to happen? I'm dying to know."

Mae shook her head. "I don't want to ruin the surprise." She gave her friend a mischievous grin. "But I'd get there early if I were you—it's going to be a packed church."

"Fine, I will. If you're ready to get up, Mae, I'll get you a robe as well as your outfit for later. That way we can all have something to eat and you'll be decent."

BEN AND MAE ARRIVED AT All Saints' that evening to see an over-flowing parking lot. Cars had been stashed everywhere, even parked on the grass. Every man, woman and child in Rosedale had seemingly chosen to attend the popular Christmas Eve service.

"I'll stop by the front door and let you out, Mae," Ben said, bringing the truck to a stop. "Don't try to get out. I'll come and help you down. Do you want the wheelchair?"

Mae gave him a narrowed-eye glare reminiscent of the looks Suzanne December often gave her husband.

"I take it that's a no," Ben said grinning, glad to see Mae's feistiness returned after her terrible fears of the night before. He walked around the car and gently lifted her down to the sidewalk.

"I'll be in the front row with my folks, July and her family. Father Brice reserved it for us," Mae told her husband.

"I understand I'm to walk our purple-coated and red-hatted Nativity thief down the aisle after the play. Once she's on the platform, I'll join you. I just wish I'd set eyes on the baby Jesus." Ben shook his head, frowning.

"Oh, ye of little faith, Sheriff," Mae said, grinning. "It is Christmas Eve you know."

THE POWER WAS FLICKERING ON and off in the church and the ushers were handing out votive candles. The lowered lighting and the scent of burning candles gave the whole scene a sense of expectancy. The entire congregation quieted as the organist began playing the lovely carol, "Oh, Little Town of Bethlehem." The children in their pageant costumes walked solemnly on stage and took their positions in front of the Nativity display that had been brought inside the church the previous night.

July's daughter, Livi, playing the part of Mary, wore a white choir robe with a blue scarf over her hair. The Three Wise Men, who varied in height from a tall ten-year old to a pair of five-year-olds, were dressed in burlap tunics and holding little jewelry boxes. The boy who had the part of Joseph was dressed in jeans and an old paint shirt. It still had a few splashes of color on it. One young girl in a white robe was trying to adjust her angel halo. Several of the smaller children were dressed in various costumes representing goats, cows, and even a rabbit. Matt Bradley in his Shepherd Boy costume stood like a proud little soldier to the right of the manger. *The backpack on his shoulder was a bit of a discordant note,* Mae thought, suppressing a giggle.

Everyone in the congregation had taken their seats when the organist began the Christmas Oratorio by Bach with its thrilling strains announcing the birth of Jesus. As the back door to the church opened, a gust of cold air blew into the sanctuary, and everyone turned to see Sheriff Ben Bradley in his dress uniform walk Mrs. Laurel Anderson down the aisle. Whispers spread through the attendees. The woman was well-known and deeply beloved in Rosedale. She was slender with pure white hair and soft pink cheeks. Her bright blue eyes sparkled beneath her red beret. Mrs. Laurel had been a dancer all her life and still moved with balletic grace. She served faithfully on every charitable initiative in the town and despite her age maintained the extensive flower garden around the bandstand all summer.

Gripping on to the end of the pew, Mae Bradley pulled herself up (with difficulty) to a standing position. Slowly the entire congregation stood with her. At weddings people always stood for the bride, but this show of respect was for the town's treasure. When Ben and Mrs. Anderson reached the dais, Father Brice extended his hand to assist her. Ben joined Mae in the front pew.

The organist stopped playing. The church was hushed. Then a voice coming from behind the stage intoned, "And it came to pass in those days, that there went out a decree from Caesar Augustus, that all the world should be taxed. Joseph also went up from Galilee, out of the city of Nazareth, into Judaea, unto the city of David, which is called Bethlehem to be taxed with Mary his espoused wife, being great with child."[5]

At this point one of the baby donkeys was led struggling on stage and tied to the Manger. The boy responsible handed

---

5 https://www.bible.com/bible/1/luk.2.4

him a carrot and he settled down. Mary and Joseph took their places in front of the manager as the voice continued saying, "And so it was, that, while they were there, the days were accomplished that she should be delivered and Mary brought forth her firstborn son, and wrapped him in swaddling clothes, and laid him in a manger; because there was no room for them in the inn."[6]

Matt walked to center stage holding his shepherd's crook. Mae could tell he was scared, but he squared his shoulders and tapped the stage three times with his crook.

The voice continued, "And there were in the same country, shepherds abiding in the field, keeping watch over their flock by night. And, lo, the angel of the Lord came upon them, and the glory of the Lord shone round about them: and they were sore afraid."[7]

There was a brief scuffle behind stage and a spotlight clicked on. It wavered a bit, but was adjusted and shone directly down on Matt, the Shepherd Boy and a little angel who had joined him.

"And the angel said unto them, Fear not: for, behold, I bring you good tidings of great joy, which shall be to all people. For unto you is born this day in the city of David a Savior, which is Christ the Lord. And this shall be a sign unto you. For you shall find the babe wrapped in swaddling clothes, lying in a manger."[8]

July's daughter Livi took Matt's hand and together they knelt down by the manger. Matt unzipped his backpack, and pulled out the baby Jesus figure. He turned around and held it aloft so the congregation could see. A series of smiles and whispers passed through the worshippers. Ben glanced over at Mae with raised eyebrows.

"Put him in the manger, now," Livi whispered audibly. Matt laid the baby down and stepped back as the speaker's voice continued, "And suddenly there was with the angel a multitude

6  https://www.bible.com/bible/1/luk.2.6, 2.7

7  https://www.bible.com/bible/1/luk.2.8, 2.9

8  https://www.bible.com/bible/1/luk.2.10, 2.11

of the heavenly host praising God, and saying, Glory to God in the highest, and on earth peace, good will toward men."[9]

The organist began to play "Joy to the World" as the little angel took center stage and a shower of silver confetti fell on her from the balcony overhead. All the children, except for Matt and Livi, moved offstage. Mrs. Anderson walked over to the podium and picked up the microphone. The spotlight was adjusted to shine on her. She cleared her throat and began.

"For those of you who don't know me, my name is Laurel Anderson and I plead guilty to being Rosedale's Nativity Thief. With the blessing of our beloved priest, I will now tell you what inspired my actions." She took a breath and continued. "Earlier this fall, I had a minor incident with a teenage boy who was looking at his phone. He didn't see me and ran into me on the sidewalk. He yelled at me, saying I should watch where I was going, and besides bruising my shoulder, it really shook me up. It was then I started noticing a worrisome pattern of events in our community." She stopped speaking and looked around at the congregation.

"As most of you know, my mother ran a dance studio in Rosedale for many years. I started coaching the little dancers when I was sixteen and Myra Cooper was six years old. She impressed me right from the start with her total lack of coordination or any sense of timing," Mrs. Anderson shook her head, and some in the congregation chuckled quietly. "Despite her handicaps, Myra never gave up and continued to dance, albeit badly, until she graduated from high school. When I heard rumors that she may have been killed because of her refusal to vacate her house on Columbia Street, despite pressure from the property developers, I was not at all surprised. Her courage in the face of adversity was the hallmark of her character and her life. Her death was the catalyst that inspired me to give Rosedale a 'wake-up' call.

"I walked by All Saints' one evening to see the Nativity Display and noticed that the spotlights were off. That was when

9  https://www.bible.com/bible/1/luk.2.14

the idea of stealing the display came to me. With no lights on, it would be possible to steal the figures undetected. All the figures were originally brought to my carriage house while we decided where we were going to hide them. A few days later, a dear gentleman friend of mine passed away while at the Senior Center. At his funeral I learned that he could have been saved if Mayor Oustelet," she paused and looked directly at the Mayor who shifted uncomfortably in his seat, "had kept his promise to fund a Nurse Practitioner position for the Center. It was then I decided to hide the figures at places in the community where promises had been broken.

"After hiding the Three Wise Men at the Senior Center, I discussed where each of the other figures should be hidden with my housekeeper who volunteers for Animal Rehab. She told me the place almost had to close because of an unfunded grant from All Saints." Mrs. Anderson looked directly at Father Brice then. He flushed and bowed his head. "So, we left the Shepherd's Boy and the donkeys there.

"Furthermore, my gardener is dying of cancer. He was one of the Hospice patients who signed the letter to the hospital CEO pleading for a last look at the Christmas tree Rosedale General had promised to plant in the meditation garden. We decided Joseph would be left where the tree should have been installed. Since then, I'm happy to report Joseph has been returned to All Saints and the tree has been planted.

"I was still deciding where to put the other figures when my hairdresser told me her granddaughter had chosen to have her baby at the Angels Birthing Center. That Center is for women who choose natural childbirth and the facility does not use epidural pain meds. Her granddaughter had a particularly long and painful labor during which she requested a transfer to Rosedale General. Her request went unanswered because, although the Fire Department's contract with the birthing center promised to provide ambulance service twenty-four-seven, no ambulance was available for her." She paused and her mouth tightened as she looked at the Fire Chief who frowned at the ambulance driver sitting beside him. "Mother and baby are doing well now, but the mother had to spend two weeks in the hospital after the birth.

"Finally, my cook's husband was recently hospitalized. When she went to pray for him at the hospital chapel, she found its doors locked and bolted." At this, Mrs. Anderson locked eyes with the CEO of the hospital who looked positively humiliated.

"Sadly, it seemed to me that all our respected institutions and leaders—our Mayor who governs our community, All Saints' where Father Brice tends to our spiritual well-being, Rosedale General Hospital where our health is maintained and the Fire Department that runs our ambulance service had all failed to live up to their promises. I could hear the bonds of civility and respect in Rosedale shattering." Mrs. Anderson looked straight at the congregation. "It was then the rumors about Myra Cooper's death reached my ears.

"That was when I called together the Angels of Rosedale. They are all with us today," she smiled. "But I won't ask them to stand until I can be reassured that they will not be prosecuted." She looked at Ben who nodded and gave her a thumbs up. Seven men and women, most with gray hair, rose to their feet. There was prolonged applause before Laurel Anderson resumed speaking. "Although I was the Commander for the mission, it was the Angels who stole the Nativity figures in the dead of night, all except for the baby Jesus. I personally wrapped the figure of the baby Jesus in reeds, just as baby Moses had been, and placed him near the pond behind the elementary school. I hoped a Good Samaritan would happen upon him. And these two children did," she said, smiling at Matt and Livi. "By taking such drastic actions, I sought to remind everyone in our community that promises kept are the exemplars of our love for one another. I ask you to remember on this holiest day in the Christian calendar the immortal words of the poet Robert Frost who wanted to stop his horse by the woods to watch it fill up with snow, but could not. He said, 'For I have promises to keep and miles to go before I sleep.'"

The congregation were silent as the organist began to play softly.

"Now, before Father Brice says the prayer and calls us up for Communion, I wonder if anyone has any questions."

"Miss Nativity Thief, I do," Matt said in a quavering voice. "Is it okay if I take the Baby Jesus out of the manger and put him back in my backpack now? I want to give him to my Dad for Christmas."

"I'm sorry, Matt, but I can't grant your wish. In all good deeds there is a sacrifice involved. Your sacrifice will be to leave the baby Jesus here. Are you willing to take this noble action?" Matt nodded, eyes wide, looking impressed. "I'm sure your father will understand, won't you, Sheriff?"

"Yes ma'am," Ben said, grinning. He stood up, stepped onto the dais, patted his son on the head and gently escorted Mrs. Anderson to the pew where she took a seat next to Mae.

The organist began to play "Away in a Manger," and Father Brice asked for a moment of silent prayer for Mrs. Anderson who he called the Conscience of Rosedale.

Mae turned to Mrs. Anderson and whispered that she was sorry, but she and Ben had to leave immediately.

"Why is that, dear?" the Conscience of Rosedale whispered back.

"Because my water finally broke." Turning to Ben, Mae whispered, "Honey, it's show time."

# TWENTY-FIVE

———— ∿ ————

MAE MOVED AS FAST as she could down the aisle, watching her husband's retreating back sprinting away from her.

"I'll pull the truck up, wait inside!" He whispered. "The steps are icy."

July limped to Mae's side, taking her sister's arm and supporting her. "Is it really happening this time?" She asked in a quiet voice.

"My water just broke." Mae gasped as a contraction hit. She stood still for a second to catch her breath and then moved forward into the cold draft that came from the open church door where her husband waited. Ben took her other arm and he and July helped her down the steps and handed her up into the truck.

Mae watched through the window as Ben and July exchanged a few words. He climbed in and turned on the flashers and the siren.

"July said she'll gather the family up and they'll be in the waiting room outside Labor and Delivery," he told her with a reassuring smile, right before he hit the gas.

Rosedale, holiday lights glowing in the falling snow, went by in a blur as Mae tried to remember the breathing exercises, she had learned in her childbirth classes. They were outside the Emergency Room entrance before it seemed possible. Ben put the truck in park and opened his door.

"Wait," Mae reached out to grab his arm. "Did we bring the hospital bag?"

"Don't worry. I put it in the back of the truck weeks ago. Stay there and I'll be right back with a wheelchair."

"Wait!" She said again. "Could you turn off the lights and siren? And what about my ID and my insurance card?"

Ben flipped the siren and flashers off and climbed out. "Your insurance card and ID are in my wallet," he said, and closed the door.

Left alone in the quiet darkness, Mae felt the wave of another contraction flow through her. Once it passed, she caught her breath. The wait was almost over and soon she would hold her babies. Ben opened her door and he and an orderly settled her into the wheelchair.

"I'm Ryan," the orderly told Mae. "I'll take you upstairs while the sheriff gets this truck parked, okay?"

"That's fine."

Lucy waved as Ryan wheeled Mae past the ER admissions desk.

"I'm taking this Mom-to-be upstairs, Dr. Ingram," Ryan said. "Dad will be right in to fill out the paperwork."

*Mom, I'm about to be a mom.* Mae smiled back over her shoulder at Lucy as Ryan pushed the elevator button. Once the elevator doors closed, she looked up at the orderly. "I'm having twins, you know," she told him.

Ryan bit his lip. "I kind of thought you might be," his eyes were kind as he gazed down at her belly. "Do you have other kids at home?"

"I have a six-year-old stepson."

"I bet he's excited about these babies, isn't he?"

Mae nodded as the elevator doors opened onto the controlled chaos of a Labor and Delivery Unit on Christmas Eve. Vanessa, a nurse she recognized from her last visit to the hospital, hurried out from behind the desk, taking the wheelchair from Ryan.

"Her husband's on his way. Good luck, Mrs. Bradley." He stepped back onto the elevator with a wave.

"Your doctor's on call tonight, Mrs. Bradley," Vanessa told her as she pushed Mae's wheelchair down the hall. "Dr. Ingram called up here when you came in and we've already paged him. Dr. Geller is on his way."

"Please call me, Mae," she told her, then bit her lip as another contraction gripped her.

The next few minutes passed in a blur of questions as the nurses helped Mae settle in. Ben skidded around the corner and entered the room to find her in bed wearing a bracelet and hospital gown. Vanessa put a matching bracelet on Ben and explained that the babies would be given bracelets as well.

"It's for security reasons," she said. "And also, to avoid any mix-ups. I always say all newborns are beautiful, but they do tend to look alike. Now, Dad, if you'd step outside for a minute, I'm going to get monitors on your babies in-utero. Use the hand sanitizer every time you enter the room, please."

Ben nodded, dropped a quick kiss on Mae's head, and left the room.

"Was he supposed to have your bag with him?"

"I bet he left it in the truck." Mae said, shaking her head.

Vanessa winked at her. "He's just excited. As soon as I get the monitors hooked up, I'll send him out to get it. If you take your jewelry off, I'll give it to him for safekeeping."

Mae removed her earrings and necklace, then regarded her swollen fingers with dismay. "I'm not sure I can get this ring off," she murmured.

Vanessa took the bottle of hand sanitizer and squirted it onto Mae's ring finger. "Now turn it sideways."

The ring popped right off, and Vanessa put all the jewelry in a plastic bag on the counter before washing her hands and placing the monitors. She then hooked Mae up to an IV and bustled out of the room, saying "Doctor will be here soon."

Ben returned with her bag and sat in the chair beside her bed. The contractions were taking on a life of their own now, three in a row separated by five or six minutes. There was a knock on the door and Dr. Geller came in. He checked the monitors and smiled at the anxious couple.

"The babies are doing well," he said. "You're progressing but it's probably going to be a while yet. How are you feeling, young lady?"

"Oof," Mae said. "That one was a doozy, but I'm okay."

"You'll probably be in transition soon," the doctor said. "I'll be checking in on you from time to time." He looked at Ben. "If she seems angry or agitated, try not to take it personally, all right?"

He turned to leave as Mae felt another contraction—and a surge of righteous anger. "You're worried about his feelings?" she yelled at the doctor. "I'm the one who's in labor here!"

"And right on time," Dr. Geller said with a smile. "Let's get your epidural going and maybe we'll get these babies out before Christmas." He slipped quickly from the room.

Vanessa returned with the anesthesiologist, and soon the pain retreated. A different orderly came in and moved Mae's bed into the delivery room. Ben was briefly detained to put on a hat and gown, but soon appeared at her side. She grabbed his hand.

"I can still feel the contractions," she said. "But it doesn't hurt anymore."

His pupils were huge in his bright blue eyes. "That's good," he whispered. "I love you."

"I love you too."

Dr. Geller examined her under the blanket that was draped over her lower body. "Do you feel like pushing, Mae?"

"I think I do." She looked up at Ben. "I think you better get down to the business end of the table."

Ben's eyebrows flew up. "Yes, ma'am." He kissed her hand and went to stand beside Vanessa, who was positioning Mae's feet in the stirrups.

"No video, right?" the nurse asked him.

"I wanted to, but she said no."

"Mae," Dr. Geller said, "on your next contraction, I want you to push. Ready?"

"Ready, another one's starting." She took a deep breath and bore down, panting through it, feeling powerful and calm. *My body knows what to do.*

"Good job." The doctor's brown eyes met hers and she focused on them with the intensity of a laser. "Just keep doing that through every contraction. Twin number one is lined up perfectly."

Twenty minutes passed and Mae was sweating and growing tired when she felt a different kind of pressure and bore down hard once more.

"There's the head, and the shoulders, it's a girl!" Ben announced triumphantly. A brief moment passed while Mae held her breath, and then she heard her daughter cry and tears poured down her own face.

Ben appeared beside her. "She's kind of messy, but perfect!"

"She really is," Vanessa said. "I'll get her cleaned up and weigh her, then you can hold her for a minute before you get back to work."

The nurse brought Mae her baby and laid the baby on her tummy on Mae's chest. She was tiny and bright pink, squalling vigorously.

"It's so good to finally meet you," Mae said. At the sound of her mother's voice, the tiny infant stopped crying.

"She weighs four pounds, eleven ounces," Vanessa said. "Time of birth was eleven-nineteen pm, December twenty-fourth. You better take her, Dad, round two will happen soon." The nurse expertly shifted the baby into Ben's arms. She took a washcloth and wiped the sweat and tears from Mae's face. "You're doing great, Mae. Try to rest for a minute, while you can."

Mae tore her eyes away from Ben and their new daughter

to close them for what felt like a second.

"Wake up, honey," Ben whispered. "They're going to give you a little oxygen now."

She opened her eyes. "Where's the baby?"

"She's in the bassinet right over there, don't worry, she's fine." Her handsome husband brushed the hair back from her forehead, then stepped back so Vanessa could administer oxygen.

As soon as she took the oxygen away, Mae asked, "How long was I asleep?"

"About half an hour."

Dr. Geller came to the other side of her bed. "Your labor has stalled, so we're going to give you some Pitocin in your IV. That should get things moving again." He glanced at the monitor. "Everything's fine right now, but I'd like to get the other baby delivered before it's stressed. The contractions will be fast and intense, so be prepared."

"That's fine. Let's do it." Mae was emphatic.

Vanessa tapped into the IV line and soon Mae was riding a tsunami wave, barely able to take a breath between contractions and trying to push. Ben started to move to the other end of the bed and Mae grabbed his arm.

"Stay with me," she gasped, and he swallowed.

"Of course."

She strained forward with one last heroic effort as Ben rubbed her back. Dr. Geller smiled and held up baby number two.

"A little smaller, but another perfect baby girl," he said, as her wails filled the room.

"I think this one's even louder," Mae mumbled, slumping back onto her bed. "Is everyone still in the waiting room?"

"They are, even Matt and Katie," Ben's grin couldn't be contained. "And Merry Christmas, by the way."

"Yes," Vanessa piped up. "Baby girl Bradley number two weighs four pounds and two ounces, born at twelve-fifteen on December twenty-fifth."

"Give her to me," Mae laughed. "I think I've waited long enough." She held out her arms. "Ben, go tell the family that Noelle Grace is here to join her big sister, Joy Malone."

Vanessa placed baby Noelle on Mae's chest and cranked up the back of her bed. Just like Joy Malone, Noelle Grace stopped crying as soon as she heard her mother's voice, crooning softly, "Merry Christmas, little one."

ON A SUNNY MORNING TWO days later, Mae was wheeled to the front of the hospital to be taken home. The air was cold and crisp when they emerged onto the sidewalk. Mae had a blanket-wrapped baby in each arm. A nurse walked on either side of her, an orderly pushed her wheelchair.

"I hope my husband was able to get the baby car seats," Mae said to Vanessa.

"I reminded him yesterday," she said.

Ben was standing at the curb in front of his truck. He wore a wide smile on his face.

"Did you get the baby seats?" Mae asked.

"Oh, I sure did," Ben looked proud.

The nurses went into action, lifting the babies from Mae's arms and fastening them into their seats. Noelle Grace gave a little cry, but then there was silence. Once Mae got into the front seat of the truck, she turned around to see two infant car seats—both pink.

"Congratulations, Mae," Ben said quietly.

"Oh, Ben, I'm so happy. Everything we talked about and wanted for our lives has come true."

"Twice over, I'd say," Ben laughed.

After a few minutes of blessed silence in the truck while the babies slept, Mae said, "But in the face of all our blessings, I don't want us to forget the Conscience of Rosedale and our need to keep our promises in the community. It's what holds us all together. So, I officially promise to be the best mother I can possibly be, to the twins and to Matt."

"While I doubt that I'll be as good as you are, I promise to be the best father I can be, and the best husband," Ben said. "I also promise to be a Sheriff you can be proud of."

"You already are, Ben." Mae looked at him with love and complete trust. "I know you'll keep those promises, just like you kept your promise that the Nativity display would be returned to the church by Christmas Eve."

HE SMILED AND REACHED OUT. They held hands all the way home.

# ACKNOWLEDGEMENTS

WE WANT TO ACKNOWLEDGE THE "usual suspects," especially Jennifer McCord, Associate Publisher and Executive Editor, Camel/Epicenter and Phil Garrett, President, Epicenter Press/ Aftershocks Media, Coffeetown-Camel Press. Both Jenn and Phil are fine editors and shepherds of our books. We especially appreciate Jennifer's work that has resulted in three of our mysteries now available as mass market paperbacks from Harlequin. Will Schkiorra has continued to be our webmaster, part-time while he's in college. The MSU Writing Group continues to provide helpful feedback. We also want to acknowledge friends, family and our children who have been very supportive of our efforts to write this final chapter that closes out the Mae December mystery series.

LIA FARRELL IS A MOTHER-DAUGHTER writing partnership. Lyn Farquhar, the mother, writes both mystery and fantasy. Lyn is a grandmother, a great grandmother, an avid gardener and a dog lover. She's a retired University professor. Lyn lives in Michigan.

LISA FITZSIMMONS, THE DAUGHTER, IS a designer and writer, mother of two children and a grandmother. Lisa lives in Tennessee where the stories in the Mae December Mystery series are set, and has a summer home in Northern Michigan.

For more information go to www.liafarrell.net